Rainbow Garden

Patricia M. St. John

Revised by Mary Mills

Illustrated by Gary Rees

MOODY PUBLISHERS
CHICAGO

©PATRICIA M. ST. JOHN 1960
FIRST PUBLISHED 1960 BY SCRIPTURE UNION
THIS REVISED EDITION FIRST PUBLISHED 2002
SCRIPTURE UNION, 207-209 QUEENSWAY,
BLETCHLEY, MILTON KEYNES, MK2 2EB, ENGLAND

THIS REVISED EDITION © MOODY PUBLISHERS 2002

Also available as an Ebook: 978-1-57567-717-0

All Scripture quotations are taken from the *New King James Version*. Copyright © 1982 by Thomas Nelson, Inc. Used by permission. All rights reserved.

Cover design: Ragont Design
Cover Illustration: Matthew Archambault

ISBN-13: 978-0-8024-6578-8
Printed by Color Hourse Graphics in Grand Rapids, MI – 7/2017

We hope you enjoy this book from Moody Publishers. Our goal is to provide high-quality, thought-provoking books and products that connect truth to your real needs and challenges. For more information on other books and products written and produced from a biblical perspective, go to www.moodypublishers.com or write to:

Moody Publishers
820 N. LaSalle Boulevard
Chicago, IL 60610

9 10

Printed in the United States of America

Contents

1. Land of Sunshine   7
2. The Welcome   14
3. The Other Side of the Mist   25
4. The Foot of the Rainbow   32
5. Stirrings Under the Snow   39
6. The Stranger in the Garden   47
7. Through the Open Window   54
8. The Rainbow Shell   61
9. In the Beech Wood   69
10. Into the Light   77
11. Easter Sunday Morning   83
12. Philippa Comes Home   88
13. A Difficult Visit   96
14. A Birthday Remembered   104
15. A Sudden Meeting   113
16. The Child at the Door   119
17. The Camp by the Lake   126
18. Philippa's Day   133
19. A Shock and a Meeting   140
20. The Rescue   147
21. The Path that Led Home   155

Revised Edition

It is over forty years since the first edition of Patricia St. John's *Rainbow Garden* was published. It has been reprinted many times and has become a classic of its time.

In this new edition, Mary Mills has sensitively adapted the language of the book for a new generation of children, while preserving Patricia St. John's skill as a storyteller.

1

Land of Sunshine

It all began one cold January night when I was kneeling in front of my mother's fireplace, drying my hair. Outside, the snow was falling over London, and the footsteps and the noise of the traffic were muffled, but inside my mother's pink bedroom, with the velvet curtains closed and the lamps casting down rosy light, we were very warm and cozy.

I was enjoying myself, for it was one of those very rare evenings when my mother was at home and seemed to have nothing to do except be with me. This was so unusual that at first we had not quite known what to say to each other, but we had watched television, and then she had brought out a pile of magazines full of patterns and had let me choose a new summer dress. After that, she had washed my hair and dried it while I watched in the long mirror and ate chocolates.

It should have been a lovely evening. Mrs. Moody, the housekeeper, had a day off and had gone home to Golders Green, and the flat somehow seemed brighter without her. I was fond of Mrs. Moody, who looked after me far more than my mother did, but she was not a very cheerful person to have around. She disapproved of Mummy because she went to so many parties and stayed out late at night and got up late in the morning. Mrs. Moody, in her young days, went to bed at ten and got up at six, and no nonsense, but as Mummy usually went to bed at two and got up at ten, I couldn't see that she was really any lazier than Mrs. Moody. They both spent exactly the same number of hours in bed.

Mrs. Moody disapproved of me, too, because she thought I had too many party clothes and too many cream cakes for tea. I had heard her tell the cook in the flat downstairs that I would grow up to be a butterfly like my mother. The cook had replied that, for all my fine clothes, I was a plain little thing; but I didn't understand what she meant.

"Mummy," I said, tossing back my hair and looking up at her, "you still haven't told me what day I'm going back to school. It must be soon now."

My mother was silent for some minutes, and I began to wonder what was the matter. I had asked twice before, and she had changed the subject.

"When, Mummy?" I repeated impatiently.

Instead of answering this simple question, my

mother suddenly said, "Elaine, would you like to go to the country?"

I twisted my head around and stared at her. "The country?" I repeated. "Why? Where? Do you mean instead of going to school?"

"Well, no," replied my mother, "not exactly. I mean, you'd go to school in the country, and I'm sure you'd love it when spring comes. The thing is, Elaine, I've got the offer of a marvelous job; but it means travelling about and going abroad and I just can't take you with me."

"Well," I said, after thinking it over for a few minutes, "I think I'd rather stay here with Mrs. Moody. I'd be at school all day, and we'd be all right in the evenings. You'd be home for the holidays, wouldn't you?"

"But, darling," answered my mother rather impatiently, because she always liked everyone to agree with her plans at once, "you don't understand! We couldn't possibly afford to keep the flat and Mrs. Moody just for you. You'll simply love it in the country, and there is such a nice family who is willing to have you. They've got six children, and there is a girl called Janet who is only a few months younger than you."

"But if you give up the flat and Mrs. Moody," I said blankly, "where will my home be? I mean, I won't belong anywhere."

My mother gave a little shrug of annoyance, and I knew she thought I was being naughty and difficult, but I couldn't help it. I didn't particularly mind Mummy going, for I never saw her much in any case.

But Mrs. Moody and the flat were a different matter. I would be like a stray cat and not belong anywhere. Besides, if I did go to the country and didn't like it, or if those six children turned out to be horrible, where would I come back to?

"Don't be silly, Elaine," pleaded my mother. "Of course when I come back we'll get a new home, and you'll always belong to me. Do try to be sensible. I don't want to leave you, but it will be much better for you later on if I earn more instead of what this part-time job I've been doing pays. Besides, I've always wanted to go abroad, and this is a marvelous chance."

I sat staring into the red glow of the fire, my mouth closed in an obstinate line. Six children in the country sounded horrible to me; I didn't want to go at all.

My mother was quite annoyed by my silence. She started again in a coaxing voice.

"You've no idea how nice it will be," she urged. "And I've taken such trouble to find a really nice place for you. Mrs. Owen was at school with me and, although we lost touch, I liked her better than any other girl I knew. Then when your daddy was killed, she wrote to me. She saw the news of the plane crash in the paper, and she wanted to know all about you and asked if she could be of any help. Of course, you were only tiny then, but I wrote to her a little while ago and asked if she knew of a nice boarding school, and she answered by return mail, offering to have you in her home so that you could go to school with her daughter Janet. It was very, very good of her, Elaine, and you must try to be a sensible girl. France isn't far away, and I will come over and see you from time to time."

I just sat silent, but I could see her face by glancing in the mirror, and it was clear that she was worried and frowning.

"Elaine," she said suddenly, "I'm going to have a little party tomorrow night to say good-bye to a few friends. You can help me get it ready, and then you can put on your best party dress and come to the beginning of it. Won't that be fun?"

I looked up quickly. "Tomorrow? Already?" I cried. "Then when are we going?"

"Well," said my mother hesitatingly, "there'll be such a lot to do packing up the flat, I thought you'd better go fairly soon. I told Mrs. Owen you'd go on Friday."

Friday! I thought to myself. *Today is Tuesday— just three more days!* I suddenly felt terribly lonely, but I wasn't allowed to say no, and it didn't seem much good making a fuss when it was all settled. Nor did there seem to be anything else to talk about, so I escaped as soon as I could and crept away to bed.

The next day was busy, and I almost forgot my fears in the preparations for the party. The guests were coming at 8:30, and by half-past seven I was all ready in my best dress with my hair carefully curled. I had never been to a grown-up party before, and I wondered what we'd do.

I was disappointed on the whole, for although everyone made a fuss of me to begin with, they very soon forgot about me. There were no other children, and we didn't play games, although I think they were going to play cards later on. They sat about eating and smoking and making jokes I couldn't understand. I began to feel dizzy from the heat and smoke and rather sick from all the cakes I'd eaten. Mummy was busy pouring drinks, and I didn't think anyone would notice if I went away.

I slipped out and went into the kitchen. Mrs. Moody at least had not forgotten me. She was sitting in an armchair mending my clothes. "Come along, Elaine," she said sharply. "It's time you were in bed. You're half asleep!"

I still felt sick and leaned up against her. "Come with me, Mrs. Moody," I whispered. "I feel sick!"

"I'm not surprised, such goings-on at your age," retorted Mrs. Moody, getting up at once. But she put her arm around me very gently and led me to my room and helped me get ready for bed. Then she fetched me a hot-water bottle because I was shivering.

"Mrs. Moody," I said suddenly, "I'm going to the country, and Mummy's going to France."

"So I understand," she replied stiffly.

"Mrs. Moody," I whispered, "have you ever lived in the country?"

A slow smile spread over Mrs. Moody's face. "I was brought up in Sussex," she said, "in a little cottage with a garden full of lavender and sweet peas and roses. To my mind, it's a better place than London for children."

I snuggled closer. It sounded like the nicest kind of story. In my imagination I could see Mrs. Moody as a little girl, thin and straight-backed and solemn, with her hair pulled back behind her ears.

"Go on," I whispered. "Tell me more."

She gave one of her rare little chuckles. "I can't remember much about it now, Elaine," she said, "except the swallows making nests under the thatch and the stream where we used to play, all goldenlike, and the posies we used to pick. My granddad knew the names of all the wildflowers."

A burst of laughter exploded across the passage. I nestled closer to Mrs. Moody. We seemed shut in by ourselves in a world of happy memories.

"Mrs. Moody," I said pleadingly, "why don't you come with me?"

"Because I'm not invited, love," she answered, "and you're a big girl now. I've got another job as housekeeper, but I shall miss you, dearie, I really will."

"Tell me more about the country then," I said, and she chatted on about lambs and cows and fruit picking and orchards. I felt cool and well again, and I lay listening until I fell asleep.

2

The Welcome

The next day flew by, and my mother was kinder to me and took more notice of me than ever before. She spent a lot of time with me and took me out shopping, and in the afternoon we had tea at a "posh" hotel and went to a pantomime. It was really exciting, and in the daytime I almost forgot about Mrs. Moody, who sat faithfully in the kitchen, sorting and marking and letting down my clothes. Only at night, when Mummy left me with a hurried kiss and went out for the evening, did Mrs. Moody become important.

It was not difficult those last nights to persuade her to come and sit by my bed in the dark and go on talking about the country. This was a good thing, for it was only after dark that I began to feel that the world was really a very unsafe place and that in a very short time I would really belong to nobody. I would be shut up with six children whether I liked them or not, and whether they liked me or not, and down at the bottom of my heart I knew that the children at school did not like me much, and I sometimes wondered why. No one had ever told me that I was spoiled and vain and cared for no one but myself—except Mrs. Moody when she was cross, and I had never taken any notice of her.

However, Mrs. Moody said that the countryside was such a lovely place to be, I felt a bit comforted by the thought of it. I had only been to the seaside in August for my holidays, and I had imagined that I was going to be taken away to a bright world of flowers, where the sun shone every day. This was a nice idea, for the snow had melted in the London streets, and the pavements were thick with brown slush and the air was heavy with fog.

Mrs. Moody remembered more and more as the week passed. She told me about harvests and hay fields and sheep-dipping, and I would lie listening, clinging to her hand and feeling comforted. When at last the dreaded morning came and the taxi stood at the door to take me to Euston station, I realized with dismay that it was far worse saying good-bye to Mrs. Moody than to Mummy. When we turned the corner and I lost sight of her thin figure waving on the doorstep, I felt that I had suddenly been cut off from everything that made life safe, and I burst into tears.

My mother, who was in the taxi with me, was upset by my sobbing and begged me to be good and sensible; so, as usual, I dried my tears and kept my fears to myself. At Euston we went to the book stall and bought some of my favorite comics and two big boxes of chocolates, one for me to eat in the train and one for the Owen children. This cheered me up, and when the whistle blew and the train steamed off, I was able to wave quite cheerfully. In fact, I was impatient to be off so that I could settle down to enjoy the journey—and the chocolates!

Mummy had asked a lady to keep an eye on me, but I was not a friendly sort of child and, since I took no notice of her, she soon gave up trying to take notice of me. I read my comics and munched my sandwiches and chocolates, and now and then I went and stood in the corridor and looked out of the window. What I saw filled me with dismay, for this country was nothing like Mrs. Moody's country. It was miles of wet, yellow fields and bare black hedges and trees, with the distances blotted out by mist. It looked cold and muddy and lonely and miserable, and I soon got tired of it. I curled up in my corner and went fast asleep.

If it hadn't been for the lady looking after me, I would have slept right through the stop where I was supposed to get out. She woke me just in time, and I tumbled out with my big case and stood waiting on the platform, still half asleep and very bewildered and cold. The train roared away immediately, and the first thing I noticed was the quietness—no traffic or footsteps, only the muffled sound of the sea on the other side of the station and the soft rattle of waves breaking on pebbles, and when I sniffed I found that the air smelled salty and clean.

Just as I realized that the sea was only a few yards away, I looked up and saw a woman hurrying toward me as fast as the three little children clinging to her hands and coat would allow, and one was only a toddler. They had been waiting for me at the far end of the long platform, and I supposed they were the Owens. I did not go forward to meet them, but stood quite still by my case.

"How do you do, Mrs. Owen," I remarked stiffly, trying to imitate my mother's voice when she greeted visitors she didn't like, and I held out my small, gloved hand.

Mrs. Owen hesitated, surprised, and there was just a second's silence as we stared at each other in the dim light of that January afternoon. Then a look came into her face that I did not understand—she might have been going to laugh or cry; in any case, she ignored my hand and kissed me very gently on both cheeks.

"How nice you've come, Elaine," she said. "We've all been so excited, and Peter and Janet were so cross they couldn't get home in time from school to meet you. But Johnny and Frances and Robin have come, and the others are waiting at home. Now come along —the taxi's just outside."

Johnny and Frances and Robin seemed as doubtful of me as I was of them and they had hidden behind their mother. I suppose they expected me to speak to them or kiss them, but I knew nothing about little children, and they were much younger than me any-way. In their woolly hats, overcoats, and strong country shoes, they all looked as wide as they were tall. When we reached the taxi, they all tumbled into the backseat and started whispering to one another under a blanket. I sat in the front with Mrs. Owen and just answered yes and no to her questions, feeling very shy and lonely.

The landscape, once we'd left the town, was the gloomiest I'd ever seen in my life. It was a cold, drizzly evening, and the trees were blotted out. I could see nothing but wet roads, yellow fields, black hedges, and not a soul in sight. Whatever did people do here all day?

I stopped listening to Mrs. Owen and stared out of the window. The little ones kept peeping out from under the blanket like rabbits, and giggling and disappearing again. I think it was their way of trying to make friends, but I took no notice of them.

"There's our house," cried Johnny suddenly, poking me rather painfully in the back and pointing ahead, and I followed his finger, suddenly interested. We had been driving between trees, but now we were out in the open country again, and there on the hillside beamed the uncurtained windows of a house that stood on its own; the windows looked warm and friendly and welcoming. I glanced timidly at Mrs. Owen, and she smiled.

"Welcome to the vicarage, Elaine," she said. "Here we are, back home."

As the taxi pulled up at the gate, the front door was flung open, and two sturdy children and a big collie dog tumbled down the path making a great noise. I hated noisy, rough children and shrank back into my corner. But they didn't seem to notice, for they were prancing excitedly around their mother. When at last I did climb out, the dog leaped up and put his front paws on my shoulders and tried to lick my face. The children shrieked with delight, for this was apparently what they had taught him to do, but I thought he was going to bite me, and I screamed with terror. Mrs. Owen rescued me in a moment and calmed the commotion.

"He's just greeting you, Elaine," explained Janet, "and he can shake hands too. Hold out your hand, and he'll hold out his paw. He's a very polite dog."

But I thought he was a horrible dog and backed away, which surprised the children, for they could not imagine anyone being afraid of Cadwaller. I saw Janet and Peter glance at each other in amused surprise as we somehow all made our way up the garden path and in the front door. It was clear I had made a bad beginning.

"You are sleeping with me," said Janet kindly, making another attempt at a welcome. "I'll show you where and help you unpack." She led the way upstairs, and Peter came behind, carrying my case. She flung open the door of a little bedroom with two beds side by side.

I was not pleased, nor did I pretend to be. In London I had had a bedroom to myself with a fireplace, and a thick carpet on the floor, and my own little oak bookcase and armchair and toy box. This seemed to me a cold, shabby little room, and I did not notice all the tokens of welcome around that the children had prepared so carefully—the hyacinth on the chest of drawers, Frances's favorite teddy sitting on my bed, Peter's favorite picture stuck on the wall above my pillow, and the little moss garden arranged in a tin lid on my chair.

Janet watched me eagerly, but I gave no sign of pleasure, and after a moment the expectant look died from her face. She shyly pointed out my bed and drawers and said she'd better go and help her mummy get supper. I felt she was glad to leave me, and I was glad to be left. I looked distastefully around at the rather shabby bedside mats and faded curtains and bedspreads, and then I noticed two sticky boiled sweets and a faded sprig of winter jasmine lying on my pillow. I flung them angrily into the wastepaper basket. Mummy and Mrs. Moody would never have allowed rubbish to be left on visitors' pillows, and I didn't see why Mrs. Owen should either. I opened my case and began hanging up my dresses in the closet that I was to share with Janet, and I was pleased to see that my clothes were much nicer than hers. I laid out my new nightie in full view on the bed; perhaps I could show her a thing or two, even if I was frightened of dogs.

But just as I was arranging the frills on my night-dress, Mrs. Owen came in and sat down with the youngest member of the family on her lap—a round bouncing baby of ten months with big blue eyes.

"This is baby Lucy," said Mrs. Owen, "and I hope you like babies, because I'm counting on your help. Six children is a lot, and you'll be my eldest girl. You are eleven, aren't you?"

"Yes," I answered, staring at baby Lucy. It had not

occurred to me that I would be expected to help. At home Mrs. Moody did all the work, and I amused myself or watched television or read books. I was not sure if I liked the idea or not; helping with a baby might be fun. In any case I could try, and if I didn't like it, I wouldn't do it, for I intended to be happy in my own way. And to me happiness meant having what I wanted and doing what I liked.

I followed Mrs. Owen down to supper, after watching her tuck baby Lucy in her cot, and was relieved to see that a large potato pie was carried in by a rosy-cheeked girl called Blodwen. I was afraid they had no maid, and that I might be expected to wash up or dust, which I would not have liked at all and had no intention of doing.

When the meal was ready, Mr. Owen appeared from his study. He was a tall, round-shouldered man with a tired face and kind blue eyes. He picked up Robin, who had flung his arms around his father's knees and nearly sent him flying, and greeted me very warmly. Then he said grace and we sat down to a noisy meal, for Janet and Peter had not seen him since breakfast and there was a lot of news to share. Johnny and Frances seemed to have done a great deal since dinnertime and were bursting with news.

"Dad," began Peter, who had only gone back to school that day, "I'm sitting next to Glyn Evans in class, and he said he'd swap me two rabbits for some stamps and a catapult—can I, Dad?"

"Daddy," broke in Janet, not waiting for a reply, "I might be in the under-twelve netball team; do you think we could put up a post in the garden so I could practice shooting?"

"Can I, Dad?" said Peter.

"Daddy, Daddy," squeaked Johnny, suddenly remembering and going rigid with excitement, "we stood on the bridge when the train went underneath, and all the smoke came up around us."

"Could I, Daddy?" persisted Janet.

"There were two baby lambs in the field; I heard them cry," said Frances in a whisper that reached her father's ears above all the noise. She smiled broadly at him, confident that her bit of news was perhaps the most exciting of all, and he smiled back at her.

"Can I, Dad?" said Peter again. He was a very persevering boy, as I discovered later.

"Could I, Daddy?" said Janet at the same moment.

"Why, yes, I think so," answered Mr. Owen peacefully. "There's an old post in the garage—Jan, we could fix it up with some wire. And I'll see if I can find a box and some netting for your rabbits, Pete. What about you, Elaine? Do you play netball?"

"I used to sometimes at school," I mumbled, wishing they would leave me alone. I felt terribly shy with all these happy, confident children, and I wished Janet wasn't so keen about netball. I'd never liked games much. I'd sat at home on the holidays or gone to shops with my mother, and I'd never learned to run about and jump and play.

I didn't like the potato pie either; it was too thick, and I wanted to go home. My eyes filled with tears that might have fallen, but I suddenly realized that Frances was looking at me in a secret kind of way, her homely little face alight with excitement.

22

"Did you see them?" she suddenly whispered across the table while Peter and Janet had a loud discussion about what kinds of rabbits they wanted.

"What?" I whispered back shyly.

"Them—my surprise," she answered softly, her eyes shining. "What I put on your pillow—did you see?"

I suddenly remembered the sticky sweets and the withered twig. I had thought them rubbish, but now they suddenly seemed precious. They showed that one, at least, of this rowdy gang had cared about my coming.

"Yes, I did," I answered. "I did. Thank you, Frances."

Then it suddenly became quiet, and I noticed that Johnny had laid a Bible in front of Mr. Owen. He was about to read, and a strange sort of calm seemed to settle over those restless, eager children. I had always thought the Bible was a very dull Book, but tonight everyone appeared to be listening, even little Frances.

I did not attempt to listen, for I was certain I couldn't understand it if I tried. It was something about a vine and some branches, but only the last verse caught my attention.

"These things I have spoken to you . . . that your joy may be full."

I thought about these words, for I liked the sound of them. Then everyone shut their eyes and bowed their heads to pray, and this I understood, for Mrs. Moody sometimes made me say the Lord's Prayer: "Our Father in heaven." But in a moment I realized that this was different, for Mr. Owen seemed to be speaking to Someone who was really there, and we all seemed to be in a place of safety—Mummy far away in London, the children around the table, the babies asleep upstairs—we were all brought near to Someone who cared for us.

An hour later, when Mrs. Owen had kissed us good night and Janet had fallen asleep beside me, I lay awake, staring out of the window at the starry sky that looked so wide without any roofs and spires massed against it. I felt quite bewildered by all that had happened, and it seemed ages since the taxi had turned the corner, hiding Mrs. Moody from view. Once again my eyes filled with tears of loneliness, and I wanted to go home—and yet there were those strange words that seemed to comfort me a little: "These things I have spoken to you . . . that your joy may be full."*

What things? I wondered.

I wished I'd listened.

* John 15:11

3

The Other Side of the Mist

When I awoke the next morning, Janet, fully dressed, was roaming around the room getting ready for a Saturday at home, and the moment she saw my eyes open she started talking. Her shyness seemed to have vanished overnight, and while I dressed, she sat on her bed jigging up and down and telling me about all their games and secrets. By breakfast time I had stopped wondering what people did all day in the country. In fact, I couldn't think how these children managed to crowd so much adventure into twelve short hours.

Breakfast was over, and everyone had helped and seemed to enjoy it. Janet and Frances fought for the job of feeding Lucy, and I was afraid she might be pulled in half. But Mrs. Owen put her head around the door and reminded them that it was Frances's turn.

The boys had gone off to bring in firewood, Mrs. Owen had gone into the kitchen, and it was suddenly very quiet. There was no sound at all except the gurgly sounds of Lucy eating her breakfast. I stood looking out of the window; it was a drizzly day, and I could see nothing beyond the garden gate except yellow fields and black trees. The distance was blotted out by mist, and I wondered what I would see when it lifted. I was startled out of my daydreams by the touch of Mrs. Owen's hand on my shoulder.

"Elaine," she said, "when you've made your own bed, will you come and help me with the little ones' beds? And then the children want to go out and play, and I expect you'd like to go with them."

I looked up surprised and not very pleased. For one thing, I did not see why I, as a visitor, should be expected to make my own bed—Mrs. Moody always made it at home. Also, what would we do out-of-doors on a cold, damp day like this? But I had learned, in my short life, to keep silent about what I thought, so I followed Mrs. Owen upstairs and started to make the beds. But I had been used to central heating and fireplaces, and I found the bedrooms horribly cold. I shivered and looked sulky.

"It is cold in the country compared with London," said Mrs. Owen, "but you'll soon get used to it. You need to run about and keep moving, and you'll get as rosy as Janet. This is the bleakest time of the year, you know, Elaine, but spring is on the way. Every day is getting longer and lighter, and we shall soon have the flowers coming out. You'll love it then."

And then suddenly she started talking about my mother at school, and that was really interesting. I listened eagerly and laughed, and felt quite disappointed when the noise downstairs in the hall told us that the children were ready to go out.

Johnny came crashing upstairs in his boots. "Mummy," he shouted, "I found a dead rabbit and we're going to have a funeral. Have you got a shoe box?"

"Really?" said Mrs. Owen rather anxiously. "Not a very dead rabbit, is it, Janet?"

"No, Mummy," answered Janet reassuringly, "a just-dead one—it was still warm."

"Well, don't touch it," said their mother, hurrying down with newspapers and a broken cardboard box. "Wrap it in this paper and some big leaves, and put it in here. There, now, don't touch it again; and Johnny, wash your hands."

"I'm not playing funerals," announced Peter grandly. "It's a game for babies. I'm going tree-climbing."

"Oh, no, Peter," cried Janet, "we always play something with the little ones first. You needn't be in the procession. You can go and dig the grave and ring the bell, and I'll be the priest. We must do what the little ones like sometimes. We'll climb trees afterward."

Janet, as I discovered later, adored funerals and wouldn't have missed it for anything, and the moment Peter had gone off to do as he was told, she started organizing things.

"Get leaves and jasmine, everyone," she ordered, "and make the box pretty."

She was interrupted by Robin bursting in. He didn't know what a funeral was, but he was terrified of missing it.

"You can drive the shoe box, Robs," said Janet kindly. "Jumbo can be a black horse with plumes, and we'll tie the box to his tail with string. I'll be the taxi driver and come behind with Francie and Johnny in the wheelbarrow. Oh, there's Elaine too! I forgot her. You can walk behind and carry flowers, Elaine."

"There aren't any," I said coldly. I thought they were all quite mad.

"Get a yew bough, then," said Janet, pointing to the tree by the gate, "and let's start. Peter's getting angry."

We went very slowly because Jumbo, a strange, shapeless, stuffed woollen animal with four legs, a trunk, and a tail sticking in all directions, was being walked step by step down the path with the box thumping behind him. Peter banged the dinner bell impatiently from behind a hedge.

I was surprised at what I saw around the corner of the hedge. There was a neat little animal cemetery with tiny graves surrounded by pebbles and marked with wooden crosses. On some the names had been carved with a penknife and filled in with ink. There were graves for thrushes and rabbits, a squirrel, a mouse, and Blackie the kitten, and at the far end a freshly dug hole lined with laurel leaves and all ready for the poor rabbit, who was laid carefully inside. Frances sprinkled a few daisies, then it was covered up. Janet said a few words about rabbits and they all sang a hymn.

"Come along now," said Janet. "We'll find Peter and go to the tree. We've got some plans to make."

She picked up the wheelbarrow and gave Robin and Jumbo a ride, and I followed. Only Frances lingered, making daisy chains for the new grave. She loved the little cemetery, for to Frances the grave was nothing but a door into heaven where nothing was hurt or killed or destroyed. But of course I knew nothing about this at the time.

Mugs of hot chocolate and ginger biscuits were served out of the kitchen window at this point, and then we all set out again, leaving Robin under the kitchen table with the cat and collecting Cadwaller from his place. Cadwaller was not allowed at funerals, for once he had tried to eat the rabbit who was about to be buried.

Peter had gone on ahead and we hurried after him, joined at the gate by Frances. We ran along a muddy path and found him already seated on a low bough of a beech tree, dangling his legs and carving the bark with his penknife. He called to us to hurry, saying that he would be working on his rabbit hutch all afternoon, and there was no time to spare.

"Frances first," ordered Peter, lying flat on his tummy along the branch. Janet gave her a lift, and Peter seized her hands and pulled. Once astride the branch, tiny Frances climbed hand over hand up into the tree like a nimble squirrel. Johnny did the same.

I was seized with horror, for I'd never climbed a tree in my life and was certain I never could.

"Come on, Elaine," said Peter kindly. "You can easily reach alone. Jump, kick your legs, and wiggle around."

But I knew I could do nothing of the kind. I would make a fool of myself and get hurt. I turned my back on him.

"No, thank you," I called over my shoulder. "I don't like climbing trees; it's babyish. I'm going home to unpack."

I did not turn around to look at them, but there was complete silence for a moment or two. Then Peter said, "Oh, never mind her, Jan; she's too stuck-up for us. Jump, and I'll give you a pull."

I walked home slowly, half blind with tears I was too proud to let fall. *These children,* I thought, *will never like me.* I would never like them or their silly baby games, and I felt terribly sorry for myself.

"I hate the country, and I hate Peter," I muttered to myself. "I shall write to Mummy and tell her I'm very, very unhappy, and I want to go home at once. I won't stay in a place where I'm unhappy. Why should I?"

I had reached the top of the little slope, and I glanced backward. The four children were sitting on a high bough dangling their legs like a row of happy monkeys. They were all very close together and probably all talking at once. How stupid they were!

But as I looked, I noticed something else. The sun had begun to scatter the mist and was shining brightly, revealing a beautiful country landscape with the sea in the distance. On a holly tree nearby, a robin puffed out his breast and sang for joy, and his breast was as scarlet as the berries. Everywhere I turned I could hear chirps and twitterings of the birds waiting for spring. For a moment I felt almost happy.

But how could I be happy when no one bothered about me, and I couldn't do what I liked? My eyes were blinded with tears—yet the robin kept on singing.

4

The Foot of the Rainbow

I shall never forget my first Sunday in the country.

Sundays at home had been rather miserable. Mrs. Moody went to a meeting somewhere, wearing a big black hat, and came back in a bad mood. Mummy nearly always stayed in bed all the morning and went out after tea. I had often found it a long, lonely, boring day.

But here everyone dressed up in their brightest and best clothes, and I learned to my surprise that we were all going to church. We set out at a quarter to eleven along a muddy footpath that led through fields, with the birds singing in the mist. Peter had gone ahead with his father, and I was glad of that for I really disliked him very much indeed. Janet skipped nearly all the way, and Johnny and Frances clung to their mother's hands, both talking hard all the time but not expecting any answer.

I walked apart on my own, wishing I didn't have to go to church. I was sure it would be really boring. We soon reached the wooden gate where people were waiting to greet Mrs. Owen, whom they all knew and loved. While they were chatting, I noticed something that made me gasp.

The old churchyard was covered with masses of snowdrops. I moved off to see them more closely, and forgetting everyone, I bent down to examine them. They were spotlessly white and so beautiful. They were clumped particularly thick around an old gravestone, and I started reading the words on it:

"David Davies—1810–1880. In . . ."

But the next words were completely worn away. Only with difficulty could I make out the end:

". . . is fullness of joy."

I had heard those words before! They were like the verse Mr. Owen had read at the tea table. What could the missing words be? Where could this "fullness of joy" be found?

But as I stood there dreaming, Janet suddenly gave me a friendly thump on the back. "Come on, Elaine," she said. "We're going in."

We marched to our pew and Johnny smiled at everyone. After a certain amount of shoving and scuffling, we all settled down, and the service began.

I didn't even try to listen. I kept repeating over to myself the words I had read in the churchyard— "fullness of joy . . . fullness of joy."

I felt that these words held some tremendous secret, and perhaps the missing words were the key. In where, or in what, could "fullness of joy" be found? And what was "fullness of joy" anyway? Nothing I had ever known in my dull, lonely little life, and yet something I was crying out to know. Then, as I stood there, something happened. The sun pierced the mist outside, and the church was suddenly filled with a golden light, warming and blessing us all. Everyone lifted their faces in amazement at this miracle of sunlight, and I glanced at Janet, who was singing at the top of her voice.

Just for a moment I thought I knew what "fullness of joy" must be like. It would change everything, even the ugly things, and make all the ordinary things precious and beautiful. But just as I made that discovery, a cloud blew across the sun, and the church was plunged into shadow again.

By the time we came out, it was raining again, and we raced home at top speed. Cadwaller came bounding to meet us and tried to leap up and greet us with muddy paws on our best coats, and we were all very warm and rosy by the time we reached home.

After dinner it was still raining, so we settled in front of the fire to play games or read until we went out again to Sunday school at a quarter past three. The box of chocolates I had brought were handed around, and I was glad to see it, for at home my mother was always giving me sweets and chocolates, and I ate them whenever I liked. But here they seemed to appear only after Sunday dinner or around the fire after supper, and seemed a special treat.

It took a long time to decide who was to have which chocolate, but at last quiet settled over the room. I was at a table writing to Mummy, but I couldn't think of much to say. "Dear Mummy," I started, "please come and take me home again. I don't like it here, and the children don't want to play with me, and it's horribly cold." I sat biting my pen and gazing out into the garden, wondering what to put next. The rain was still falling, but it was a bright, thin rain with the promise of sunshine behind it. As I watched I suddenly noticed one of the brightest rainbows I'd ever seen in my life. The children round the fire with their backs to the window noticed nothing, and I did not say anything. It was my rainbow, and I wanted it to myself.

I had read stories about treasures hidden at the foot of rainbows, and the foot of this rainbow was just up the hill. It seemed to touch the earth behind an old stone wall, and although I no longer believed in fairy stories and hidden treasure, I thought it would be fun to run and stand in the light with the colors breaking all over me.

I got up quietly, shut my writing pad, and walked to the door. To my great relief, no one asked me where I was going—they were not very interested in me. My coat was hanging in the hall and I slipped it on, turned the front door handle very softly, and escaped.

I trotted up the hill feeling the soft rain on my face, with the rainbow, which was fading a little now, still ahead. By the time I reached the wall where its foot had rested, it had disappeared altogether and the sun had come out.

I stood still, looking up at the wall where the foot of the rainbow had been. It had ivy hanging over it like green curtains, and it looked secret and exciting. I followed it until it turned a corner, and then again around another corner, and this time I found a green wooden gate. By peering through the cracks in the boards, I could see a little gray stone house set in a garden, and the windows of the house were all shut tightly with dark blinds drawn down over them.

I pressed down the latch of the gate very carefully, but it was locked. The house seemed quite empty, and perhaps no one lived here. The garden where the rainbow had rested was a secret, deserted garden, and I suddenly wanted to get inside more than anything else in the world.

There were tall trees growing all around the inside of the wall with branches trailing over it. Peter and Janet would have clambered over in a minute, but to me it looked almost impossible. I wandered along, searching for footholds, and very soon I came to a hawthorn bush with a broken bit of wall behind it, and there were easy footholds. I scrambled to the top quite easily, swung on an apple bough that seemed stretched out to welcome me, and landed with a thud on the muddy lawn. It was the first time in my life I had ever tried to do anything like that, and if anyone had been watching me I wouldn't have even dared to try.

I stood very still, rather frightened by what I had done and at first hardly dared to move. But the voices of the birds encouraged me, for the garden was full of them. It was an untidy garden covered with dead leaves. The flower beds were choked with weeds, but the snowdrops grew in clumps everywhere.

I stepped forward cautiously and examined the house. Yes, it was quite empty. The windows were locked and dark, and there were great dusty cobwebs clinging across the front door. It seemed no one had lived there for a long time.

Then I turned to the garden again, wondering just where the foot of the rainbow had rested, and suddenly I knew—there, on a rising mound of lawn, clear of leaves, where a few yellow buttercups were still curled in tight balls.

I had often seen snowdrops for sale on street carts and around the roots of trees in the parks, but I had never seen them like this. I doubted if they grew anywhere else in the world except in "my garden," and I sat there for a long time, with the pale January sun warming my damp hair and turning the flowers a brighter gold. Never, never had I been in such a wonderful place.

Gradually I grew bolder, and I explored my kingdom from end to end. I decided to tell no one; I would come here and play all alone, and then it wouldn't matter that I couldn't climb trees or play their silly games. And one thing I had discovered helped me a great deal. Lying against the back of the house was a half-rotten piece of ladder, which I dragged across the lawn and propped against the wall. It took my light weight quite well, and I was able to get out of the garden quite easily.

I had no idea how long I'd been there, or what would be said about where I had been, but the sun was beginning to set behind the western hills and the birds had nearly all stopped singing. Only a late blackbird, perched on an apple tree, sang on.

"Fullness of joy" it seemed to sing, "fullness of joy . . . fullness of joy."

5

Stirrings Under the Snow

The family had started tea when I got home, and Mr. Owen had gone out to look for me. The children, as usual, were in a great state of excitement.

"Where have you been?" shouted Janet. "Daddy's gone to look for you, and you missed Sunday school."

"We thought you had drowned in the river," remarked Johnny cheerfully.

"Or you'd been kidnapped," added Frances, her eyes very round.

"Or we thought perhaps you'd run away," chimed in Peter, his mouth full of cake.

"Where've you been?" demanded Robin, beaming at me over his mug of milk.

There was one good thing about these children: they asked questions so hard and fast that there was never time to give an answer or explain, and I did not wish to explain. I looked rather anxiously at Mrs. Owen to see if she was cross; she had certainly looked relieved when I came in.

"You mustn't go so far alone till you know the way about, Elaine," she said gently. "The paths are confusing around here. Now stop asking where she's been, all of you. She doesn't know where she's been. She only came the day before yesterday."

Nevertheless, as soon as tea was over, she called me into the kitchen and, sitting down on a chair by the window, she pulled me gently toward her and asked me herself where I'd been.

"Only for a walk," I replied rather rebelliously. "There's nothing wrong in going for a walk alone, is there, Mrs. Owen?"

"Oh, no," she said quietly, "there's nothing wrong at all. Janet often goes for walks alone. It's just that I'm afraid of you getting lost when you don't know the country. Come and tell me when you want to go out alone, Elaine, and then I shall know where you are."

I was rather surprised at this speech, for I had thought she was going to be cross, but she wasn't at all. Yet she seemed puzzled, as though she was trying to understand why I would want to be alone, and I had a sort of feeling that if I could make her understand, she would try to help.

"Mrs. Owen," I murmured, "do you see that wall?"

She gazed out into the dusk. Over the hills above "my cottage," there were still orange streaks in the

40

stormy sky, and I could see the wall.

"Yes?" she answered questioningly.

"Well," I said, "I won't go any farther than there. Just around the other side of the bushes there's a special place where I want to play. And please, Mrs. Owen, let me go and play there alone, and don't let the others come and look for me. I like playing alone better."

She smiled understandingly, for she knew all about special places. All of her children had them.

"You can play there whenever you like, dear," she said kindly. "You've been used to playing alone, haven't you? All the same, I hope you'll sometimes play with Janet and Peter too. They'd like you to share their games."

I didn't answer and, having got what I wanted—permission to play alone—I drew away. "I haven't finished my letter to Mummy," I said stiffly, and went back to the table, where I tore up my effort of the afternoon and started again. "Dear Mummy," I wrote, "I hope you are well. I like it in the country, and I would like to stay here a long time."

I stopped writing; what would my garden look like after a long time? Perhaps it would grow into a garden like Mrs. Moody's, full of pansies and roses and lilies, and I would watch it grow all by myself. I forgot my letter and sat dreaming.

But it was a whole week before I went back to my garden, for the next morning I started school, which took up most of my time and attention. I found the sturdy Welsh children different from my elegant friends in London, and I kept to myself, although kindhearted Janet did her best to look after me and drag me around with her. But Janet was extremely popular and was always losing me and forgetting me in the merry crowd of girls she went around with.

By Tuesday there was a strange white light in the sky, and by Wednesday snow had started to fall, and when we came out of school it was inches deep on the hills. The children went mad with joy and all started snowballing each other. I got one right down my neck and, not being used to snowballing, I lost my temper at once and got really angry. Janet, red in the face with shame, apologized, but the other girls giggled and drew away from me. "She's no fun," said one of them, and the game went on, but no one else threw snowballs at me. From that moment I was out of it.

Janet and I tramped up from the bus together in silence, miserable and shy of each other. As we reached the gate, Peter, who was home before us, burst out of the house.

"Come on, Jan," he shouted. "I'm going to help Mr. Jones bring in the sheep. I met him on the way up, and he says if we don't hurry some of the ewes will be snowed up in the ditches, and he thinks there's one going to have lambs tonight. Give your bag to Elaine and come quick!"

Janet, relieved to get away from me, swung her bag onto my shoulder and dashed up the hill after Peter. They did not invite me to come, too, I noticed, but actually I would not have wanted to even if they had, for my fingers and toes were numb with cold and my collar was wet from the snowball. I let myself in and went up to my bedroom, sat down miserably on my bed, and stared out of the window.

Big snowflakes were floating down from a low gray sky, and I imagined the drifts were already piled against the wall of my garden. I began wondering what it looked like inside now. I wondered if the snowdrops and buttercups were buried so deep they would die. And as I sat there hoping they wouldn't and gazing out into the white world, Mrs. Owen came in.

"Why, Elaine," she cried, "why are you sitting there for in your wet clothes? You must change your shoes and socks and come down by the fire. You'll catch your death of cold sitting in this icy bedroom! Where's Janet?"

"Gone with Peter to bring in sheep," I answered. "Mrs. Owen, do flowers die when the snow buries them?"

She was already pulling off my socks and rubbing my numb feet with her strong, warm hands.

"Dear me, no," she answered. "There are wonderful things going on down under the snow. One day of sunshine will melt it all and the next will bring the flowers out in a rush."

I smiled in spite of myself, for I had a sudden vision of the flowers pushing up so fast that I could see the petals unfolding. Besides, my toes were beginning to feel as though they belonged to me again, and up the stairs crept the delicious smell of hot toast. I felt comforted and went down to tea with my hand in Mrs. Owen's.

The snow lasted for two more days, and Peter and

Janet spent most of each evening up at the farm. On the second night, Mrs. Owen asked them to ask me, too, so I went with them. Dusk had already fallen, and the sheep were all settled down in the barn where the ewes were brought when their lambs were born. One had had triplets that very morning, and Mr. Jones had been up most of the night with her. Now she lay peacefully on a heap of straw, her job happily done, and two tiny lambs nuzzled her for milk.

"Where's the third?" asked Janet, squatting beside them.

"Here," replied Mr. Jones with a chuckle, holding up a crumpled fleece. "It was born dead. I skinned it right away."

"What are you going to do with it?" asked Peter.

"Now, you've come just in time to see," said Mr. Jones, and he strode across the snowy yard with Peter and Janet at his heels. But I stayed where I was, watching the lambs and their tired mother, for I liked the barn with its smell of sheep and leather and paraffin and straw. The light had faded outside, and Mr. Jones had lit the lantern.

The lambs had finished feeding and lay curled as close as they could to their mother; it was a cold world to have tumbled into, and they were very small and crumpled. Outside a fox barked, and some strange night bird answered with its hunting cry, but the lambs only pressed a little closer against the ewe. Neither snow nor darkness nor night hunting could hurt them. They were safe and warm and satisfied.

I heard crunching footsteps in the snow outside,

and Mr. Jones came in with the children behind him. In his arms he carried a third lamb, which snuggled against him as trustfully as the twins had snuggled against their mother.

"Look, Elaine," whispered Janet eagerly, "it's an orphan—its mother died. Mr. Jones is going to dress it up in the fleece and see if this mother will take it on."

It looked a very odd little thing when the skin of the dead lamb had been tied around it. Mr. Jones carried it up to the peaceful group in the straw and laid it very gently against the flank of the ewe. She turned her peaceful face to it and sniffed it in a puzzled way, as though looking for her dead lamb. Then she laid her forelegs protectively over it and claimed it as her own. The odd little creature snuffled and wriggled as though pleading to be accepted and then, quivering with delight, pushed its head underneath her and started to feed.

But it had to reckon with its foster brothers. They turned angrily and started butting it with their tiny heads. The frightened little trespasser wriggled away, crying and shivering, and bleated aloud for a mother. Tenderhearted Janet was down on the floor in a minute, gathering it into her arms, but Mr. Jones reached out and took it from her.

"Now, don't make a fuss over it," he said. "It's got to make its own way. I'll try again in half an hour's time. It's bigger than those twins, and it must learn to stand up for itself. Now you must be getting home, or your mother will be coming to fetch you."

We turned reluctantly from the warm, lantern-lit

barn and went out into the clean frost. It was a starry night and everything sparkled. "Race me home," shouted Peter, setting off at breakneck speed down the crunching farm track with Janet at his heels. But I was afraid to run in the slippery frost and was just about to shout after them to stop and wait for me, for it was very unkind of them to dash off like that and leave me alone in the dark. If I shouted loud enough, Janet would come back and walk with me, for she was always kind if she remembered to be.

But suddenly I seemed to see that ridiculous, dressed-up lamb crying for pity, and to hear Mr. Jones's steady voice as he picked it up. "It'll have to make its own way. It must learn to stand up for itself." It certainly did seem as though trying to make people feel sorry for you didn't get you very far in the end.

I took a deep breath and began to run—cautiously at first, but I soon found that it wasn't nearly so difficult or dangerous as I had imagined. Clumsily and with a beating heart, I began to gather speed, and as I galloped along I passed a stone wall and thought of my buried garden with its roots stirring.

"There are wonderful things going on under the snow," I murmured to myself.

6

The Stranger in the Garden

All Saturday we tobogganed and snowballed and made a snowman with some of the village children, but by midday even I, unused to the country, realized that a change was taking place. A warm south wind was blowing, and by the end of the afternoon every tree was dripping, and the grass was showing through the toboggan tracks. The poor snowman was shrinking and his hat had fallen down over his shoulders. We squelched up to the farm in our Wellington boots, and long before we reached the gate we could hear the restless cries of the lambs, who were straining to escape to the open meadows. "I'll let 'em out tomorrow," said Mr. Jones, who was sweeping out the barn. "Spring's on the way, and they know it!"

The children and Cadwaller knew it, too, and had seemed to me quite excited all day, rolling noisily about in the snow. Fortunately they had not tried to push me over, and I just stood around most of the time, feeling cold and bored. I was glad to get back to the farm and the lantern light in the barn.

"What happened to the lamb, Mr. Jones?" I asked eagerly.

"Come and see," said Mr. Jones kindly, and we squelched through the muddy slush to the door of the fold. He held up the lantern and pointed to a corner.

"See there now," he exclaimed.

The ewe was lying on her side as before, and nuzzled against her were three lambs, all feeding contentedly together. The biggest of the three seemed perfectly at home and even gave a little shove to the twin who was taking up most of the room.

"What happened?" I asked. "Did they stop butting it?"

"No," chuckled Mr. Jones, "but she stopped crying and butted back; that settled things!"

We smiled at each other, and then Peter, Janet, and I went bounding down the hill, hungry as hunters, the orange lights in the windows shining out to welcome us home. I was left far behind again, but instead of being angry, my thoughts wandered to the sleeping garden. Perhaps even now the snowdrops and buttercups were pushing up. I decided to go first thing next morning to investigate.

Fortunately I woke very early. Janet was fast asleep, and I dressed very quickly and then softly tiptoed downstairs. It was seven o'clock—two hours till breakfast. I paused for a moment on the stairs, wondering if Mrs. Owen was awake. I sped on downstairs and slipped out through the front door and didn't stop running until I was halfway up the hill; then I stopped to get my breath back.

A big thaw had set in during the night and the earth was drinking deep. I thought about the roots underground. "One day of sunshine, and everything will burst out"—that was what Mrs. Owen had said.

The sun was not up yet, but the sky grew brighter and clearer every moment, and the birds were singing joyful messages to each other. The garden, when I slipped over the wall and climbed down my ladder, was still asleep in the shadows, and the snow was piled against the house. But on the lawn it had melted, and the buttercups smiled up at me, and the snowdrops clustered stronger and sturdier than ever. I wandered in, thrilled, and turned the corner. Then I stood quite still, rooted to the spot, for a man was standing in the little yard gazing at one of the darkened windows.

I do not know if I was frightened or just very surprised. He glanced around furtively and saw me standing there. He gave a startled jump but seemed to recover at once. Walking up to me he said, "Good morning" in quite a pleasant voice.

"Is there anyone at home?" he asked rather uncertainly.

"I don't think so," I replied. "I think it's an empty house. Either no one lives there, or they've all gone away."

He frowned at me fiercely, and this time I definitely felt frightened. "Then what are you doing here?" he asked severely.

I could have asked him the same question, but I didn't think of it. I only minded about one thing, and that was that I should not be turned out of my garden, so I replied as boldly as I could, "Oh, I live just down the hill. I'm allowed to come here. I look after the garden."

He looked at me narrowly. "Thought you said you didn't know who lived here," he said after a moment's pause.

"Well," I answered, "I don't exactly know who they are because I've only just come to live here, but Mrs. Owen down the hill knows them, and she said I could look after the garden."

I didn't know whether Mrs. Owen knew them or not, nor did I care, for no one had taught me the importance of speaking the truth. But once again the man's manner changed, and he spoke pleasantly.

"Well, it's a nice garden to look after," he said, looking around. "I'm a bit of a gardener myself. Do you come here every day?"

"Oh, no," I answered. "I go to school every day. I only come here on Saturdays and Sundays."

He looked relieved. "Do you mean to tell me," he questioned, "that you see to this garden all alone? Does someone else come in during the week?"

"I don't think so," I answered innocently, for I did not like the idea of anyone else invading my secret place. But the moment I said it I wished I hadn't, for it began to dawn on me that this man shouldn't be here, and why was he asking all these questions?

I did not like him; his face looked ill and haggard and unshaven, his clothes were dirty, and he smelled of drink. Nor did I like the way he kept glancing around out of the corner of his shifty, frightened eyes. I stared at him very hard, and I think he felt uncomfortable, for he suddenly pulled his cap down over his eyes and turned away.

"Well," he said, "if the master's not at home, it's no use waiting. I'll call again. So long!"

He climbed over the barred gate and was gone, and I gave a sigh of relief and turned back to my garden. But somehow the birds were no longer singing as they had sung before. Perhaps they had just been frightened away by our voices, but it seemed to me as though some dark shadow had fallen across the garden, and for the first time I felt lonely.

But not for long. As I stood wondering whether I should run home again, I saw a streak of golden brown, and a squirrel came darting down the trunk of an old chestnut tree in the corner. He sat looking at me from between the roots of the tree, his bright eyes twinkling, and as he twitched his tail, all my loneliness melted away, forgotten.

I knew what I wanted to do that morning, and I worked away happily until the sun came up over the hill. I wanted to make a little rockery like those I had seen in parks. Someday, coming out of school when Janet was busy with her friends, I would slip away unnoticed and buy seeds. Then when summer came, my rockery would be a mass of color, and bees and butterflies would hum and flutter over it, just like in

Mrs. Moody's garden in Sussex.

So I ran to and fro, banking up the soft earth and collecting stones till it was nearly breakfast time. I noticed a ring of crocuses pushing through the grass. I jumped into it, pretending it was a fairy ring. Here, all by myself, with no one to laugh at me for being such a baby, it seemed easy to believe in such things, even though I was eleven. I stood quite still, wondering what to wish for. "I know," I said to myself. "I'll wish for 'fullness of joy.' "

So I wished, and then, suddenly realizing that it was time I went back for breakfast, I skipped off down the hill.

When I got home, I ran upstairs to brush my hair and found Janet kneeling by her bed, saying her prayers. I decided to ask her an important question since I thought it might stop her from asking where I'd been.

"Janet," I said as she lifted her head, "do you know lots of verses in the Bible?"

"Oh, yes, nearly all," she answered confidently. "Where have you been, Elaine?"

"Because," I went on, taking no notice of her question, "there's a special verse, and I know the beginning and I know the end, but I want to know the middle. It's like this: 'In . . . something . . . is fullness of joy.' "

Janet said, "I'm not quite certain, but I think it's 'In heaven is fullness of joy.' In fact, I'm sure it is; I think I remember. Now—it's time for breakfast. Come on!"

She danced away to help carry in the porridge

bowls, but I stayed behind, slowly changing my shoes. I was disappointed in Janet's answer, for heaven was far away, and I wasn't sure that I'd ever get there. Mrs. Moody had told me that good people went there when they died, but I didn't know if I was good or not, and I'd never thought about it much. I thought I was better than Janet, for I didn't forget things and I wasn't so noisy and untidy.

Yet Janet cared about people in a way I did not. I had not realized that I cared for no one but myself, but I did wonder what made Janet different. I wandered about after breakfast still thinking about it, and stood looking down curiously at the unmade bed and open Bible with the shabby little notebook inside it. What did she see in it, and what did she write down carefully every morning? I stooped down to peep at what she had just copied out in her round, clear writing.

"Be kind to one another, tenderhearted, forgiving one another, just as God in Christ also forgave you."*

* Ephesians 4:32

7

Through the Open Window

We had a week of sunshine after the snow, and spring arrived with a rush. Every day we hurried home from school, flung down our schoolbags, gobbled down our tea, and went off up the hill to play. Mrs. Owen had great difficulty making us do our homework.

The Owen children skipped and ran because they liked it, and I ran behind them because I had nothing else to do. Yet I was beginning to change. My garden had taught me the beauty and magic of the country, and scatterbrained Janet and sturdy Peter were beginning to teach me that life was more fun if you thought of other people as well as yourself. I knew now that the Bible was not just a dreary Book for grown-ups; it was about Jesus, who spent His life making sad people happy and bad people good. Sometimes I wished I could come to Him, but I did not know how, and I was much too shy to ask.

Perhaps, strangest of all, I now really wanted to be like the other children and no longer thought them stupid. Yet, although they tried to be patient, I knew quite well that they thought me stupid. My fear of cows, my slowness in climbing trees, my ignorance, and the time I took getting over a gate amazed them—I was so slow and clumsy.

At the end of March, Peter's class was taken for a day's trip by coach to the Natural History Museum in Liverpool. It was pouring when he came home, and we were all indoors. Peter burst in on us, dripping and joyful.

"Mum," he cried, "I've had a brilliant idea. I'm going to start a Natural History Museum here in the house!"

"Are you, darling?" replied Mrs. Owen, carrying on with what she was doing. "Have you had a lovely time? And have you changed your shoes?"

Peter flung wet arms around his mother's neck. "Mum" he shouted, "I'm serious! We would need a room and dozens of jam jars. Could we have the ones in the kitchen cupboard? And clear out the attic?"

"But I need them for bottling fruit," replied Mrs. Owen. "And where would we put the things from the attic? Now change your shoes and get out of that wet coat, and we'll talk about it at supper. We want to hear all about the museum."

We did hear all about the museum; we heard of

nothing else and talked of nothing else for days and days and days. We cleared all the things in the attic over to one end, leaving half the room free, and Peter put up shelves. Then one rainy Saturday afternoon, a Very Important Meeting was announced in the living room. Peter stood on a box with his hand raised for silence.

"We shall have sections and departments in this museum," he announced grandly. "There'll be the birds' egg section, and the wildflower section, and the shell section, and the skeleton section . . . and . . . fossils and butterflies and anything else interesting anyone can collect. We shall work in teams—two and two, and—"

"I'll go with Pete," yelled Johnny, flinging himself at the box and upsetting the speaker.

"Me and Jan!" shouted Frances, clutching her sister's skirt.

Peter and Janet looked at each other. "If Elaine took the little ones, Jan and I could go together."

But the little ones burst into tears, and I felt angry too. Nobody wanted me; the little ones wanted the big ones, and the big ones wanted each other. I flushed red with loneliness and hurt, and marched to the door.

"I'm not having anything to do with this silly old museum," I shouted. "It's just a baby game. I'm sick of it."

I slammed the door behind me, and seizing my coat I ran into the garden. I heard Janet come out and call after me, but I didn't stop. Tears of self-pity were running down my cheeks, and I wanted to get away from them all. I hated them.

The rain had nearly stopped, and everything smelled of wet earth and fresh growth. I had not been to my garden for over a week—there was no time with this silly museum craze—but I would go now, quickly, before all the children came tumbling out of the house and saw me.

I was up the hill and over the wall in a few minutes, and once again the peace of the place seemed to cast a spell over me. My stormy little heart became quieter, for wonderful things had happened in the garden. The almond tree was covered in pink blossom, daffodils flowered in a golden ring around its roots, and the birds sang here as they sang nowhere else. The seeds I had planted on my rockery were beginning to sprout bravely, and little honeysuckle tendrils were creeping against the stone walls.

I explored every nook and cranny. I did not know what all these things were, but I stood looking at them wonderingly, and as I did so a brown bird with a white-and-speckled breast darted from the lilac bush beside me and made me jump. And then suddenly I drew in my breath, for the hours spent with Peter and Janet had taught me that birds darting in and out of bushes sometimes meant nests.

Surely I wouldn't find a nest on my own! With a hand that almost trembled I parted the boughs and peeped in. Yes, there *was* a nest, carefully woven from twigs and moss and mud, and down at the bottom of it lay two turquoise eggs speckled with black markings.

I looked and looked, holding my breath, my temper all forgotten. How could I have thought nests boring and stupid? Now that I had found one myself, I knew they were the most precious, beautiful things in the world. Of course, Peter and Janet would want to see it if I told them, but I wasn't going to tell them. It was my own secret, and I wasn't going to share it with anyone.

Then as I sat watching, the thrush with the speckled breast started singing from the top of the almond tree. I imagined it looking straight at me.

"It's our own secret," sang the bird, "me and you . . . me and you . . . we'll keep it together . . . me and you . . . fullness of joy!"

I laughed out loud and then sat down quietly on a stone to wait for the bird's return. I stared at the daffodils and the clumps of primroses against the house. If only I could stay here forever, where I felt good and happy! If only I didn't have to go back to those hateful children who didn't want me! Tears of self-pity ran down my cheeks again at the thought of them, and I suddenly found myself longing for my mother—my pretty, careless mother, who had never seemed to want me very much either. In fact, no one really wanted me. All my life I would be lonely and unhappy, and I felt so terribly sorry for myself that I forgot all about the bird and just stared in front of me. Then suddenly I noticed something so interesting that I forgot to feel sorry for myself and got up to investigate.

I ran toward the house to see better. One of the locked windows on the ground floor had been broken and opened and the curtains taken away. Where

I had only peeped before, I could now look right in, and everything was different. The chest of drawers was open, and things were spilled all over the floor. It looked as though someone had been searching for something in a great hurry.

But what caught my attention most of all was something I had not been able to see when the curtains were drawn. It was a china cabinet in the corner full of beautiful shells. I longed to see them more closely, and then suddenly realized that there was nothing between me and them. The window was open at the bottom, and I had only to give a little jump and a pull and I'd be inside. But what if anyone found me? That would never do. With a pounding heart I tiptoed all around the house, peeping into the other ground-floor windows. But they were all locked as before, with the blinds pulled down.

I tried the back door and the front door. They were locked, and cobwebs straggled across the cracks. No one had been in, and the gate was locked. I was safe to do as I pleased, and yet I did not feel safe. The garden suddenly seemed lonely.

Very cautiously, and with many backward glances, I pulled myself up and planted my muddy shoes on the sill. Then I gave a jump and landed with a frightening thud on the boards. Picking myself up, I tiptoed over to the glass cabinet and opened it, fascinated by the shells.

I put out my hand and picked them up, one by one, and turned them over. They were rare, foreign shells and corals, but I did not know that. There was one not quite so big as the others, which seemed a different color every way I turned it. I laid it down and tiptoed into the dark passage. I stood listening for some time, then, getting bolder, I crept up the staircase.

I was going to explore!

8

The Rainbow Shell

I peeped into the first bedroom and was amazed at its untidiness. A case was open in the middle of the floor with clothes hanging over the side, and there were open, messed-up drawers. Only the last bedroom I peeped in was in any sort of order, and that was a child's room, for there was a doll's house in the corner and a family of dolls on a cot. I examined them with interest. Janet didn't like dolls, and I had missed them.

Then suddenly I realized what I was doing and decided to get out. I crept back into the room with the open window and stopped opposite the cabinet of shells. If only I could find a shell like the one with all the colors for the museum. Peter would think me cleverer than anyone and would never call me stupid again.

And then suddenly a terrible thought came to me, because I was so unhappy and so wanted to be liked. There were so many shells in the cabinet . . . if I took just that one and moved the others up a bit, no one would know. And it wasn't really actual stealing, I told myself, because shells were free; anyone could pick them up on the beach. And then Peter would be sorry he'd said I was stupid, and Janet would think I was so clever. And no one would miss it or notice it, because it was an empty house anyway.

For nearly five minutes I stood with the shell in my hand, trying to persuade myself that it really would not matter. Then I slipped it into my pocket, crossed to the window, and climbed out into the garden.

It was very still. The flowers had closed their petals, the birds had stopped singing, and I wanted to escape and run home as fast as I could. I ran up the ladder and swung myself over into the wet grass, but when I picked myself up, I almost screamed because Elwyn, the shepherd boy, was standing looking at me.

"What are you doing in that place, Elaine?" he asked slowly. "That is Mr. Thomas's house, and he did not say you could go in."

I was terrified; I felt as though Elwyn's round eyes were piercing holes in my pocket. I clutched the shell tightly and turned my scarlet face up to him.

"I'm . . . I'm allowed to," I faltered. "I'm allowed to look after the garden, that's all. I never go to the house, only the garden. Oh, please, Elwyn, don't tell.

He stared at me. He was a slow boy and would probably have believed me if I had not looked quite so guilty. He shook his head slowly. "Mr. Thomas said I was to keep an eye on the place," he remarked. "You are not to go there anymore, or I'll tell Mrs. Owen about you. It's not the first time, either—I've seen you before."

"No, no," I cried, trembling. "I'll never go there again, Elwyn. I only went in the garden." I ran past him down the hill with a pounding heart, but before I'd reached the house I'd calmed down a bit. Elwyn was such a stupid boy that he'd be sure to forget all about it, and anyhow, I'd told him I'd only been in the garden. There were dozens of shells, and no one would notice one missing. I would not dare go back and play in the garden for a time, but somehow I did not mind that, for it had suddenly become a strange and frightening place.

I stopped and stood still to think. I had to decide what I would do about the shell. It was no good giving it to them tonight, as they would know I hadn't been on the beach. I would wait till after school on Monday and slip down to the shore when Janet was chatting with her friends. I would come home later, alone, with my pockets full of shells as a gift for the museum, and the rest was easy. So I pretended to be in a very good mood when I wandered into the house, and Janet came running up to me and begged me to come with her and Peter next day. I nodded coldly and said that I had ideas of my own and would probably go alone.

But I was very silent at supper, and Mrs. Owen glanced once or twice at my pale, troubled face, and when Peter bounced out of his seat and opened the

Bible in front of his father, I felt as though I wanted to run away. I was beginning to get quite interested in the Bible, but tonight I did not want to listen.

"Let me see," said Mr. Owen, "where did we get to? It was Genesis 3 last night."

"We got up to where Adam and Eve stole the apple," said Janet eagerly, "and they hid from God."

"Ah, yes," replied her father, and he read on in his beautiful voice that made the story live. A sad, sad story of a man and a woman sent out of a beautiful garden where they had been so happy—all because they did wrong. Why had they been so happy in the garden? Because God was with them. Very simply Mr. Owen explained it, and the children sat with their eyes fixed upon their father. But I sat looking at my plate, half listening and half lost in my own thoughts. When he finished, I said I had a headache and asked if I could go to bed.

Mrs. Owen came upstairs when I was in bed and took my temperature and gave me a tablet. She stayed talking to me in her kind, motherly voice as though I was her own child, and I longed to fling my arms around her neck and tell her about everything. But of course if she knew I was a thief she wouldn't love me anymore, and she might send me away. So I just lay still and let her talk, and when she kissed me good night I half turned my head away, and she went downstairs, puzzled and sad.

But I lay awake in the dark thinking about the story, and in my sleepy mind I thought it must have been written about me. Perhaps, somehow, God had been waiting for me among the flowers, waiting to make me happy, like Adam and Eve, but I had spoiled it all. And then I remembered I would never see the eggs hatch. The rockery flowers would all grow up, but I would be shut outside and never see them. I buried my face in the pillow and wept, but when Janet came up, I pretended to be asleep.

The next morning the sun was shining and I felt better, and all Sunday I tried to be very good and helpful to make up for the night before. On Monday morning I tried to help by getting Lucy dressed, but she wouldn't let me help her. The more she kicked and gurgled, the crosser I got, until at last I slapped her. She started screaming and then suddenly stopped as Janet came into the room. She flung herself into Janet's arms and clung to her for dear life.

"You mustn't slap Lucy," said Janet indignantly, slipping her clothes on without any difficulty. "She's only a baby. Besides, she'll catch cold if you let her lie on the floor with nothing on. You really don't know much about babies, Elaine."

I didn't, and I didn't want to. I went down to breakfast hating all babies from the bottom of my heart. They were so unreasonable and sticky and noisy. I was glad to get off to school and leave them, but school wasn't very successful either. I felt restless and frightened. The moment we were let out I slipped away from the noisy group that always gathered around Janet and made for the beach.

It was not a very good place for shells, but I collected a few ordinary ones and put them into my pocket with my treasure. Then I took it out and held it in the sun. It looked lavender-colored, but when I tilted it toward the sea, it turned green. Once again I thought it was the most beautiful thing I'd ever seen, but I did not want to stop and think about it. I ran across the pebbles and pedaled after Janet, who had already started for home.

"Where've you been?" asked Janet.

"Down to the beach," I answered rather breathlessly. "I've got some shells for the museum, and I found one beauty. I've never seen one like it before."

"Show me," said Janet, putting on her brake.

I shook my head and pedaled on. "When we get back home," I called, "I'll show you and Peter together."

We raced rather recklessly along the main road and turned up the lane that led to the vicarage. I was feeling rather nervous.

Peter was home already. He was busy making a new box for his birds' eggs and only grunted as we came in.

"Come on, Elaine, show us!" said Janet eagerly. "Peter, she says she's found a very special, rare shell on the beach. Bring it out, Elaine."

"That beach is no good for shells," answered Peter, barely looking up. "You have to go a long way farther—Oh, wow! Elaine, you didn't really find that one on our beach, did you?"

"I did," I said defiantly. "If you don't believe me, ask Janet. She knows I went down after school."

"All right, keep your hair on," replied Peter, glancing at me in some surprise. "Nobody said you didn't; only it's a strange thing. It must have been washed miles and miles from some other coast. We must have a very special place for it in the museum. Well done, Elaine!"

Janet was holding it in her hands, turning it around and around to the light. The little ones gathered around, standing on tiptoe to see.

"It's like Philippa's shells in the cabinet," said Janet wonderingly. "It's beautiful, Elaine. Look, first it's pink, now it's blue, now it's mauve. We must show Daddy."

They burst into Mr. Owen's study, but I hung back uneasily. I'd often heard them speak of Philippa. She was a child from the village who had had polio,* and she'd been in a hospital all winter. But where did she live, and when was she coming back?

Mr. Owen looked at me over the heads of his excited children. "You found this on the beach, Elaine?" he asked in a puzzled voice. "It's a most extraordinary find. It looks like real mother-of-pearl. Either someone dropped it, or it's been washed by the tide right across the world. It's nice of you to lend such a treasure to the museum."

"Yes, thanks, Elaine," said Peter in a hurry, in case I decided to keep it. "It really is very good of you. We'll go and see where we can put it. It's our star exhibit."

They tumbled through the door and up the staircase to the attic. Mrs. Owen smiled kindly at me, and I gave her a sad little smile back. Then instead of going with the others, I followed her into the kitchen.

---

*Polio is an illness that can leave people unable to walk properly. Today, most people are immunized against it.

"Auntie," I asked, "where does Philippa live?"

"Why, at the cottage, just up the hill," answered Mrs. Owen. "We're hoping she'll be back soon. I heard from her mother that she was better."

I turned away and went out into the garden, and Cadwaller came up and rubbed his kind old head against my legs, as though he smelled that I was in trouble.

I knelt down on the path and buried my face in his shaggy coat and flung my arms around his neck, for Cadwaller didn't care what I'd done. I might have stolen and told lies and all the rest of it, but to Cadwaller I was just an unhappy little girl needing comfort. He put out his tongue and licked me.

9

In the Beech Wood

Exams were over, and we woke up one rainy morning to the first day of the Easter holidays. Everyone was full of outdoor plans, but an absolute downpour at breakfast time put an end to them, and we all settled down to a day at home. Mrs. Owen found jobs for all the older ones, which kept us busy for some time, and the little ones tumbled about with Cadwaller. At eleven, work was over and we all got together for hot chocolate and cookies.

Peter was making a large map of the district to hang at the back of the museum. He liked to work with it all spread out on the floor, but Lucy kept trying to stagger across it.

"I don't suppose one of you girls would do something about Lucy, would you?" he said, lifting a flushed face from his work. "Oh, look! There's a policeman coming up to our front door! I wonder what he wants. Perhaps Cadwaller has killed another hen. Quick, Cadwaller! Hide. Good dog!"

Everyone, including Cadwaller, crowded to the window to look at the policeman, so fortunately no one was looking at me. I had suddenly gone very white and cold, and there was a strange, sick feeling inside me. Just supposing it wasn't Cadwaller. Just supposing they had found out something, and it was me they were after. Just supposing Philippa had come back and noticed that her shell was missing, and Elwyn Jones had said something. I stopped supposing and slipped into the kitchen and out the back door. Whatever it was about, I felt safer out of the way.

"Where are you going without your coat, Elaine?" called Blodwen from the sink, but I took no notice. All the fears hidden away in my heart for nearly a week were rising in front of me. I ran up the hill as fast as my trembling little legs could carry me, and I did not know where I was going but kept clear of Philippa's house. I took the upper path that ran across the sheep pastures, forgetting that on that high path I could be seen from the windows of Mr. Owen's study.

I had reached the level highlands above the farm, and it had stopped raining. Wherever I looked, there were hills and valleys and steep, sheep-dotted fields. To the south I could see the purple crests of the Snowdon range of mountains. But, even in my panic, I knew that I could not reach them. I had to find a nearer hiding place than that, and I looked around furtively. To my right was a wood where we were not allowed to go, for it was a pheasant reserve. But nothing mattered now; if the police were after me it did not matter if I was trespassing or not.

I slipped between the bars of the padlocked gate, for I was a thin little girl for eleven, and I trotted along the path, too out of breath to run anymore. In spite of my fright, I could not help noticing what a beautiful wood it was. The air was full of gentle sounds. Arched boughs met overhead, and it felt almost like being in a church.

I reached a little clearing in the heart of the wood where someone had made a pile of logs, and here I sat down and tried to think. If I went too far, I knew I would come out on the road again, and I didn't want to do that. The more I thought about it, the more I felt I could not go home.

I would have to face the policeman and the shocked faces of Peter and Janet, who never told lies. I couldn't do it! They would think me wicked and terribly silly, and anyhow, what would the policeman do? I didn't know whether they sent children of my age to prison or not, but I was sure they did something to them. And what would my mother say? And Mrs. Moody?

I sat there on the logs for a long time. It must have been long past dinnertime, but I was not hungry. I was sitting so still in my fear that a squirrel began to play on the tree in front of me. A bright-eyed baby rabbit bounded through the bluebell leaves, and birds darted to and fro. Everything seemed happy and busy and fearless except me.

One thing I noticed and never forgot. It was the beauty of a little clump of wood sorrel springing out of a piece of rotten bark beside me. I broke off the piece of bark and held the whole clump in my hand. Then suddenly the silence was broken by the bark of a dog and the sound of quick, steady footsteps coming through the forest.

The police! I seemed to freeze with fear. Perhaps they were hunting me with bloodhounds and police dogs; I had read about them in a comic. I think I gave a little scream, for there was a loud answering bark of joy, and Cadwaller leaped through the trees and put his paws on my shoulders and started licking my face in welcome, and behind him came Mr. Owen. I looked up at him, gave a great sigh of relief, and burst into tears.

He sat down beside me on the log. Then he said very gently, "Why did you run away, Elaine? Were you frightened of that policeman?"

I nodded and sniffed.

"But why were you afraid, Elaine?" asked Mr. Owen. "He only wanted to ask you a few questions. But I will ask you instead, and then tomorrow we'll go and tell him the answers."

"What will he do to me?" I whispered.

"Why, nothing, Elaine," he answered in a puzzled voice. "I don't suppose you've done anything wrong. Only, you see, there's been a robbery in Mr. Thomas's house, and Elwyn Jones says you've been playing in that garden. The police want to ask you whether you've seen anyone about, and whether

72

you've noticed how long ago the window was forced open, and also whether you've been into the house, because there were little muddy footprints on the sill that belonged to a child."

I sat very still, my mind in a whirl. Was I the robber or was there someone else as well? Who had opened the windows and searched the drawers? Not me, or did they perhaps think it was me?

"Tell me about it," said Mr. Owen at last.

"I didn't open the window," I blurted out. "Honestly, I didn't. I just went in to look at the shells . . . and I just took one. I thought shells didn't matter much, because they were free and you picked them up for nothing. And they all said I was stupid, and no one wanted to go with me, and I always get left behind. And I don't know anything about birds, and I thought they'd like me if I found a shell, so I said I'd found it on the beach. And Peter was so pleased. They'll think I'm awful now. I didn't know it belonged to Philippa . . ."

I trailed off miserably. It was all out, and what would happen now I couldn't imagine, yet I felt much better.

"Please, please, Mr. Owen, don't make me go back to the police," I whispered. "Make Mummy come and take me home. I'm so miserable, and now it will be worse." I looked up at him timidly, pleading. He was looking rather sad.

"You needn't be so afraid, Elaine," he said gently. "The police didn't come to ask about the shell. They don't know about it, nor need they ever know about it. It was quite a big robbery—blankets and curtains and silver and all sorts of things. It wasn't anything to do with you. They only thought you might have seen someone hanging around the house and be able to explain about those little footmarks. There's nothing to be frightened of at all. You and I can deal with that shell between us."

"There was a man," I murmured, "once, early in the morning, looking in at the window."

"Well, then, you'll be able to help the police a lot," said Mr. Owen encouragingly. "Peter will be quite jealous of you having seen a real burglar. We'll go to the police station tomorrow, you and I, and you must tell them what the man looked like, that's all. Now let's forget about that, and let's talk about the shell. You took it because you wanted them to think that you'd found something nice for the museum, and you said you'd found it on the beach?"

"Yes," I whispered.

There was a little silence. "Did it make you happy?" asked Mr. Owen at last.

I shook my head. "I kept being afraid you'd find out," I said.

"That wasn't the only reason you were unhappy," said Mr. Owen. "You were unhappy because you'd stolen and told a lie. Do you remember the story we read the other night, about Adam and Eve?"

"Yes," I answered rather vaguely. "They were in a beautiful garden too. But I only went there to make it grow. I didn't mean to be naughty at first—there were snowdrops, and it was all quiet and beautiful and the birds sang. I didn't even pick flowers."

"Of course not," said Mr. Owen. "Mr. Thomas

wouldn't have minded you playing in his garden at all. You loved it, and you were happy until you took that shell, and then you were afraid. Doing wrong always comes between us and God, just as a cloud comes between us and the sun. The sun is still there, but we can't enjoy it. The cloud has blotted it out, and everything is cold and dark. And there is only one place in the world where we can find real happiness, what the Bible calls 'fullness of joy.'"

I jumped at hearing the familiar words and looked up quickly. "I know that verse," I whispered. "Janet taught it to me—'In heaven is fullness of joy.'"

Mr. Owen laughed. "Then Janet taught it to you all wrong," he replied. "It's far, far better than that. It's like this: 'You will show me the path of life; in Your presence is fullness of joy.' That means that anywhere in the world, here in this wood or at home in the vicarage, if you are walking along the path of life close to God, you can be perfectly happy. And doing wrong is the only thing that separates you from God. When you find out how wrongdoing can be taken away, you'll know the secret of 'fullness of joy.'"

I sat very still, for I felt I was about to make a very big discovery. I even forgot my misery for a few minutes.

"How?" I asked.

"It's a long, long story, Elaine," said Mr. Owen, "and it's the most beautiful story in the world. Jesus came to this earth as a human being just so that He could take away all our wrongdoing, which is called sin. When He died on the cross, He was punished for it in our place. If there is something between two people, and someone comes and takes it away, what is left?"

"Nothing," I said.

"Nothing between," said Mr. Owen. "Just an open way for people to come to God, because Jesus died. Nothing to stop you anymore. You can come right into His presence and find 'fullness of joy.'"

My eyes were fixed on his face. What did it mean? What did I have to do next?

But I could not ask these questions aloud; I could only wonder. Cadwaller had laid his head on my knee, and I fingered his silky ears in silence.

Mr. Owen pulled out his New Testament and opened it. "Do you want to hear how wrongdoing can be taken right away?" he asked. "It's all here, written down for you."

I sniffed and nodded. I wanted to know so badly, but I still couldn't say anything. So he read some verses aloud slowly—verses written by an old man whose eyes had actually seen Jesus hanging on the cross.

"These things we write to you that your joy may be full. . . . If we walk in the light as He is in the light, we have fellowship with one another, and the blood of Jesus Christ His Son cleanses us from all sin. If we say that we have no sin, we deceive ourselves, and the truth is not in us. If we confess our sins, He is faithful and just to forgive us our sins, and to cleanse us from all unrighteousness."*

* 1 John 1:4, 7–9

76

10

Into the Light

"What does *confess* mean?" asked Mr. Owen.

"Saying you did it," I whispered, feeling ashamed.

"Yes, that's right," he answered. "It's telling God about the wrong things you can remember and asking Him to forgive all those you can't remember, and then believing that Jesus died on the cross and took the punishment for them instead of you. And then, because there is nothing between you anymore, you can come straight to God and give yourself to Him, and His Spirit will live inside you, helping you to obey Him. Would you like to do that, Elaine?"

I nodded again.

"Then tell God about it now," said Mr. Owen. "Tell Him you believe Jesus died so that you might be forgiven, and then thank Him for making you clean inside and leading you into the light."

"I don't know what to say," I whispered.

"Then I will pray," said Mr. Owen, "and you can say it with me in your heart." So we closed our eyes, and he prayed out loud. "Dear Lord, I want to tell You about the shell I stole and the lies I told and all the things I was so afraid and unhappy about. I am coming to You because Jesus died and You promised to forgive. Please wash me whiter than snow and make me Your own little girl. Come into my heart and make me brave and truthful, so that I can put right what I did. For Jesus' sake, amen."

I opened my eyes and looked around, half expecting to see Jesus standing nearby. The wood was all aglow with sunset as we got up and set off for home, with Cadwaller bounding ahead of us.

Walking in the light, I thought to myself, *that's what it's like—with nothing hidden.* I felt brave and strong and joyful for a few minutes. But it didn't last, for soon the vicarage came into view below us, with Peter and Janet waiting for our return, and I knew what I had to do. If only Mr. Owen would not walk so fast. I hung back, and he looked down at me.

"What are you thinking about?" he asked kindly. "Are you afraid?"

I nodded dumbly.

"Then you know what you've got to do to put it right?"

I nodded again.

He gave a little smile and held my hand very comfortingly.

"Let's tell them about it together after tea," he said

reassuringly. "You'll be much happier when it's all over, and you can start again. Anyhow, it won't be as bad as you think. Peter and Janet have got a lot to put right, too, as far as I can see."

The children looked at me curiously when I came in, but asked no questions, for Mrs. Owen had told them not to. Tea would have been a silent, uncomfortable meal if Mr. Owen hadn't announced that I had almost certainly seen the burglar who had broken into Philippa's house. To my surprise, I suddenly found myself the heroine of the hour. Everyone wanted to know what he looked like, and Peter made complicated plans for catching him ourselves. After tea, Mr. Owen called from his study that he wanted to see Peter and Janet and me.

He was sitting back in his easy chair, and Peter and Janet hurried forward and sat down. I hung back, silent and afraid in the doorway, but Mr. Owen called me over. When I, too, was curled up on the rug, he said quietly, "Elaine wants to tell you something."

There was nothing for it. With a bent head I blurted out my story.

"The shell . . . I didn't find it. It was Philippa's. I wanted something for the museum. It wasn't true." Burying my crimson face in my hands, I burst into bitter tears.

"Just a minute, Elaine," Mr. Owen said. "You haven't quite finished yet. Why are you telling us about it and putting it all right?"

"Because," I sobbed, "I asked God to forgive me, and I want to start again."

"Good," said Mr. Owen. "Now you need not be unhappy anymore. We are not going to punish you, because you are sorry without any punishment. You can go now and start all over again, but . . ." and here his voice changed and became rather stern, "I want you, Peter and Janet, to stay with me. I want to tell you just why Elaine took that shell."

I crept away, not daring to look up. To my relief, the little ones had gone to bed, and Mrs. Owen was sitting alone by the fire. She smiled at me, and I sat down close beside her, too exhausted to speak but longing for her kind, motherly company.

Perhaps Mr. Owen had already told her all about it, for she asked no questions. She just began talking about all the fun we were going to have over the Easter holidays. I would have liked to stay beside her, but I did not want to be there when Peter and Janet came out of the study. So after about five minutes I went up to bed, and Mrs. Owen came up a little later and tucked me in and kissed me good night.

It seemed a long time before Janet crept softly into the bedroom. I shrank down under the bedcovers, pretending to be asleep, but I think she must have known I was pretending, for she suddenly flung herself down beside me.

"Elaine," she whispered, "don't be asleep! Listen! Pete and I are really sorry; honestly, we are."

"Whatever for?" I asked, coming up from my burrow in astonishment. This was not at all what I had expected.

"Because Daddy said it was partly our fault that you took that shell," said Janet. "He said it was all because we were selfish and only wanted each other and didn't want to share. And he read us a story in the Bible that made me cry, and I think even Pete did a bit too."

"What story?" I asked, really interested.

"Oh, a story about some people who were unkind and selfish, and Jesus said to them, 'I was hungry, and you wouldn't give Me anything to eat, and I was once a stranger, and you wouldn't share and play with Me.' And when they said they'd never seen Jesus before, Jesus said, 'It was when you wouldn't share and play with My little ones.' I'll show it to you in the morning. It's in Matthew 25. Daddy said it was like us, and you were the stranger."

Her voice broke, and she sniffed. I crept closer to her.

"It's not true," I whispered. "You often tried, but I was so cross, and sometimes I didn't want to be friends. And I know it was very wicked of me to take that shell and say I'd found it on the beach, but I just wanted you to like me."

"But we do like you," cried Janet, raising her hot little face, "and we think it was very brave of you to tell, and we really want to be friends."

"And I'm not going to be cross anymore," I whispered, "because of what happened this afternoon, you see. I expect I will get nicer."

"I know," said Janet eagerly. "I'm ever so glad about that part because I belong to Jesus, and so does Pete, and lots of times we've wanted to tell you, but we thought you'd think us silly."

"Could I read the Bible with you in the mornings?"

I asked anxiously. "You see, I don't know it like you do, and you could show me."

"That would be great," said Janet, who was feeling much happier. We lay talking until Janet fell asleep, but I lay awake, thinking back over that strange, stormy, terrifying, wonderful day. Yet here I was at the end of it, lying at peace with all the world, unafraid and forgiven. Jesus had come and lifted me up, like a shepherd carrying a lost lamb. He would stay with me forever, and in His presence was comfort and peace and fullness of joy.

11

Easter Sunday Morning

It certainly did seem as though life had started again. When I woke up the next morning, I knew that I had left my dark secret behind me forever and I was never going to be alone again. I belonged to Jesus, and I would have "fullness of joy" if I kept close to Him. That was what Mr. Owen had said to me, and now everything seemed brighter and more beautiful.

Peter was sorry for making me unhappy but couldn't show it. He was very excited about trying to catch the burglar and was very envious when I had to go to the police station to describe the man I'd seen.

My great joy those holidays was the morning time with Janet when we read the Bible together and chose a special verse for the day. It was fun, and I realized how important it was to spend time with Jesus.

The first Sunday after that never-to-be-forgotten day, Mr. Owen called me into his study just before church and gave me a parcel. I unwrapped it with excitement and found a beautiful navy blue leather Bible with gold-edged pages and pictures. Inside, on the front page, was written:

ELAINE NELSON
"You will show me the path of life.
In Your presence is fullness of joy."

I loved my Bible more than anything else I possessed, although I didn't know much about it yet. But at church we read little books that explained the passages, and Janet helped too. Some mornings we ran out into the garden and sat under the apple trees or went out in the meadows, but on Easter Sunday we awoke very early and set off to the bluebell wood. There was a carpet of blue all around us, and the air was heavy with the scent of bluebells.

"I don't remember coming here before," said Janet, stopping suddenly and looking around her wonderingly. "I don't think anyone comes here. Oh, look! There's a place with the sun shining through. Come quick, Elaine! Let's go there!"

We stood in the middle of the clearing, looking about us. Birds were singing at the tops of their voices.

"Of course!" said Janet. "It's Easter morning! And this is our church! Let's read here, Elaine. Let's read that bit Daddy once read about white robes. It was somewhere in Revelation."

We searched eagerly, and Janet found it fairly quickly and read the verses. I didn't know what they meant, but I loved the sound of them.

"What does it mean?" I asked.

"I think it means you have to be very clean inside to walk with Jesus," replied Janet. "I think it means we shouldn't join in when people get together on the playground at school and talk about horrible things and whisper and giggle. Pete says the boys are worse than the girls."

I knew what she meant, for I had often been keen to listen myself.

"I think the part about 'keeping your clothes clean' means refusing to listen and going away when they start," said Janet firmly. "I did it once, and they laughed and said I was stupid, and after that I was afraid not to join in. But from now on, Elaine, let's show them that we don't like it, because actually I think quite a lot of the girls don't. If we started, they might copy us, and in any case, we'd have each other. Let's write down that verse for today, 'They shall walk with Me in white, for they are worthy.'"

We copied the verse very carefully into our little notebooks, our heads bent low, feeling the warm sunshine on our hair. Then we got up to go, feeling sad to leave our little chapel. Suddenly, we heard a cuckoo.

"First one I've heard," said Janet, "and she's early too. Come on; we'd better run. I ought to be helping Mummy."

She sped away through the woods and jumped over the gate out into the open meadow, and I followed not far behind, for I was a much better runner than I used to be. The sun was quite high, and in the meadows all the buttercups and daisies had opened their faces to the sun. Just at that moment, it seemed almost impossible that there could be anything ugly and unclean in such a bright world.

We got home to find the family in the midst of the usual Sunday commotion of getting into their best Sunday clothes. Robin was coming to church, too, as a treat, because it was Easter Sunday. He was under the table very quietly dressing Jumbo in his best clothes.

Breakfast was great fun since the Easter rabbit had hidden hard-boiled eggs all over the garden. It took a long time to find them, and when we came in, our shoes were wet with dew and our hair windswept and untidy.

After breakfast we all set off across the meadows with Blodwen, for Mrs. Owen was staying at home with baby Lucy. The church was overflowing with people and full of Easter flowers—daffodils, tulips, and white blossoms, and the choir and congregation rose to their feet and sang victoriously:

> "Jesus Christ is risen today,
> Alleluia!"

I glanced along our pew. Robin had managed to smuggle Jumbo into church, and he was beating time with his trunk. Mr. Owen told the story of the Resurrection and how an angel of the Lord in clothes as white as snow came down and opened the tomb, and I thought of Jesus coming out in shining robes to match the angel. To walk close to Him in the path of life, sharing His fullness of joy, you would need to be very clean too. Janet was right—nothing dirty or bad could stay near that pure light.

We got up again to sing the second hymn. Peter, who was in the choir, had a solo part in this one, and his voice, clear and unbroken, seemed to soar right to the roof.

Mr. Owen glanced at Robin, and a strange look came over his face. Robin, seeing his dad, had scrambled up on the seat behind Blodwen. Holding Jumbo high above the heads of the congregation, he wiggled the elephant's little gray trunk joyfully at his father.

12

Philippa Comes Home

Next morning the mail arrived during breakfast, and there was a letter from Mrs. Thomas, Philippa's mother, saying they were coming home again on Wednesday and asking Mrs. Owen to find help to get the house ready. This caused a great deal of excitement among the children, for Philippa was a friend of theirs and had done everything with them before her illness.

I knew all about Philippa too. She lived in the house belonging to my garden and had caught polio just a year ago. She had been very ill indeed, and, although she was much better, her legs remained partly paralyzed. Her father was in the navy and was usually away, and Philippa had been in a special hospital learning to walk again while her mother stayed nearby.

"Can Philippa walk again?" asked Janet eagerly.

"Only a very little, with crutches," answered Mrs. Owen sadly, "but of course she may still go on getting better. Poor Philippa! We must do all we can to give her a big welcome, and you must show her that you still want to play with her."

Everyone around the table was happy and excited except me, for I was feeling very uncomfortable. Johnny and Francie planned to fill the room with flowers, and Janet said she was going to make some sweets. Peter wanted to make Philippa a little bedside table, if his father would find him some wood. Mr. Owen thought this was a very good idea, and they went off together to see what could be done about it.

Robin decided to lend her Jumbo for a while, which was a real sacrifice.

Peter suddenly hurled himself into the room, breathless with excitement, with Janet behind him.

"My rabbits, Mum!" he cried. "They've had babies! She's pulled all the fur off her tummy and made a nest in the closed half of the hutch. Do come and see—no, not you, Elaine and Robin—one at a time. The father eats them if too many people look at them."

"You'll have to take the father away and put him by himself, Peter," said Mr. Owen, coming in. "They often kill their babies if you leave them in the hutch. Just let Mummy and Elaine have a peep, and then give the mother a good feed of bran and dandelions and leave her alone."

I seized Mrs. Owen's hand and we tiptoed to the hutch, Robin hiding behind us. Very carefully Peter opened the door just a crack, and we saw a mass of white fur. In the middle was a pink mass of squirming, squeaking baby rabbits.

"How many?" I whispered.

"Don't know," answered Peter softly. "They all seem stuck together, and I don't like to touch them to count. We'll leave them alone for a day or two till she gets used to them. Dad, instead of a bedside table, could I make a new rabbit hutch? Then Philippa could have two baby rabbits; she could have them by the bed, and they'd be good company."

"I don't know what Mrs. Thomas would think about the smell," answered Mr. Owen, "but she could have them just outside the window, I suppose. I expect they'll make her a bedroom on the ground floor. That's a very good idea, Pete. You carry on!"

Mr. Owen went back to his study, and I ran after him and poked my worried little face around the door. To my surprise and relief, he seemed to have guessed my thoughts.

"Come in, Elaine," he said. "You're thinking about that shell, aren't you, and wondering where it is? I took it out of the museum that same night, and it's here safe in my desk. Would you like to go with Auntie when she goes up this morning to get ready, and slip it back into its proper place? And one other thing I thought of—you started to make a pretty good job of the garden, and you've got two days left in which to work hard. How about finishing off that little rockery you started and tidying it up a bit?"

I was thrilled. Somehow, I hadn't wanted to go back to the garden since I had taken the shell, but I had missed it and had wondered what my seeds were doing and whether the eggs had hatched. Now I would return, not hiding any longer. Of course it was only for two days, but it was better than nothing.

I was all ready to start, clasping the shell in one hand and a trowel in the other, when Mrs. Owen appeared. I did not look at the garden till I had put the shell safely back in the cabinet, then I ran out and explored it from end to end.

It was amazing what the April sun and rain had done. Under the weeds I could see opening buds. Tulips held up flaming cups, and forget-me-nots massed the borders. I found sweet-smelling clusters of lily of the valley among the weeds, longing for the light. Last of all, I tiptoed to the lilac bush, already in bud, and peeped at my nest. There was a rustling and a cheeping, and five yellow beaks were opened wide. I laughed softly and drew down the leafy curtain.

"They thought I was their mother, bringing a worm," I whispered to myself. "I wonder where she's gone."

The mother bird kept darting past as I knelt at my weeding, and both she and I worked hard all that day and the next. I cleared the rockery completely, and the children were quite surprised at what I'd done. I could hardly tear myself away for meals and worked till the last light faded. I was happy and sad both at once—happy because I was setting free the garden, sad because it was mine no longer. Soon it would all belong to Philippa.

On the last morning, everyone came up with Mrs. Owen to bring and inspect and arrange their gifts. Peter had worked as hard as I had, and the bright green hutch was set proudly in the middle of the lawn at the side of the house to wait for the baby rabbits. Janet arranged plates of homemade fudge in every nook and cranny, and the house was decked with spring flowers. Philippa's couch was brought up to the window, complete with Jumbo, overlooking the rockery. Everything was ready except for the garden. I still hadn't weeded around the roots of the lilac tree.

"Well," said Mrs. Owen, looking around, "I think we'd better go home to dinner. Someone's bringing them by car at about four o'clock, so we'll come up then and have tea ready."

I tugged at her sleeve. "Please," I whispered, "can I miss dinner and stay to finish the weeding?"

"All right," she answered with a smile. "I'll send Johnny up with a little picnic."

I breathed a sigh of relief. Johnny was very fond of his food and would certainly not want to stay. I really wanted to be alone with my garden this last afternoon.

Johnny came and went in a great hurry, but I was too busy to bother about food just then. I was clearing around the roots of the lilac tree when I suddenly heard the squeak of brakes outside, the opening of doors, and the sound of voices. Then I heard the latch click and realized the family had come home earlier than expected.

I dived around the side of the house like a frightened

rabbit and pressed myself against the wall. I was terrified of being caught in the garden and only hoped I could escape without being seen. But I was just in time, for the next moment I heard the delighted voice of a child cry out.

"Oh, Mummy, Mummy, the garden's alive, and we thought it would be all choked! And oh, look, Mummy, the lilies of the valley are out—and oh, look, Mummy, someone's made a little rockery!"

"Why," replied a woman's voice, "someone's been hard at work. How beautiful it looks! And look, there are—"

But she was interrupted by a yell from the child.

"Oh, Mummy, Mummy, there's a rabbit hutch on the lawn around the side of the house. Come quick, and see if there's a rabbit inside!"

I knew I was caught, and stood there looking as guilty as though I had committed a robbery, The next moment Philippa's head came around the wall.

She was small and thin, leaning on crutches, her legs supported by iron frames. But I thought she was beautiful, for her fair braids hung below her waist, and her eyes were the blue of forget-me-nots. They seemed to fill up most of her pale little face, and she stood staring at me in frightened astonishment.

"Mummy," she called sharply, "come quick! There's someone hiding behind the wall!"

Mrs. Thomas, immediately thinking of burglars, came rushing around the corner with a little cry of alarm. But when she saw how small I was, she stopped short.

"What are you doing here?" she asked sternly.

"Nothing," I stammered guiltily. "I was gardening. Mrs. Owen said I could. I live with the Owens. We all came to get ready for Philippa."

Mrs. Thomas burst out laughing. "Why," she said, "you must be Elaine, the little girl who saw our burglar! Mrs. Owen wrote and told us all about it. So it's you who has worked in our garden! Well, Philippa and I think it's simply beautiful, and you must come and welcome us inside the house. Come along, Phil; you've been standing long enough."

She took a key from her pocket, picked up Philippa as lightly as though she was a baby, and carried her into the house. She laid her on the couch where Jumbo lay waiting for her, dressed in flowery trousers and a hat.

"Oh, Mummy, the flowers!" cried Philippa. "Look at the rockery, just underneath the window where I can see it all day. Do you know, Elaine, all the time I've been in hospital, I've lain in bed and looked at a brick window and a laundry chimney. Now, sit down and tell me who made the fudge and who put this elephant here. And was there a rabbit in that hutch?"

Forgetting my shyness, I poured out all the news, while Mrs. Thomas bustled around the kitchen. At one point, she put her head around the door.

"Have you had dinner, Elaine?" she asked.

I suddenly remembered my picnic and dashed off to get it. I sat and ate my sandwiches while Philippa ate her omelette, and then we all had a cup of tea with cookies.

Mrs. Thomas got up firmly. "If the family is coming

to welcome us this afternoon," she said, "Philippa must have a rest. Elaine, we'll see you again later, and we are just thrilled with the garden."

I said good-bye to Philippa and skipped all the way home in the sunshine. The garden was mine no longer, but I felt happier about it than I'd ever felt before.

It's a funny thing, I thought, *but it's much more fun doing things for other people than just doing them for myself.* And I jumped for joy as I thought of Philippa lying on the couch, her small white face turned to the rockery.

13

A Difficult Visit

The Easter holidays raced by, and I found myself busier and happier than I had ever been. For one thing, I was getting stronger and tougher and could climb easy trees and puff along behind the others quite well. And instead of thinking that their games were silly, I was beginning to enjoy them. The beauty of the spring countryside was becoming really interesting to me, and with Janet and Peter's help, I was on the way to becoming quite a naturalist.

Then there was Philippa. The children all did their best to cheer her up but, strangely, she seemed to prefer my company to that of anyone else. Perhaps it was because we were both only children, or perhaps it was because I was less energetic than the others and found it easier to sit still. In any case, I was pleased to be the favorite for the first time in my life, and to begin with I visited Philippa every day. I went on working in the garden, too, and Mrs. Thomas gave me a patch all to myself in which to grow flowers. I loved it, and used to putter about in it with Philippa lying on a rug on the grass nearby.

One day we all went out for a picnic, and the day after that Peter, Janet, and I bicycled along the coast to look for gulls' eggs. So, what with one thing and another, it was only on the evening of the third day that I went back to Philippa.

She was lying by her open window, and I hopped nimbly in over the sill and sat down on her couch. But she didn't seem at all pleased to see me, and at first wouldn't answer when I spoke to her.

"Whatever's the matter?" I asked rather crossly. "If you won't speak to me, I'll go away."

She turned her face toward me, her big blue eyes full of tears. "Why didn't you come?" she whispered. "I've waited two whole days all by myself, and you just forgot about me. You don't care about me a bit."

"I do!" I answered rather impatiently. "I didn't forget about you at all. We were just busy. I'm sorry, honestly, I am, Phil, but we went to the caves and down to the sea, and Peter and Janet wanted me to go with them, and . . ." I stopped, for she had buried her little white face in the pillow and was sobbing bitterly.

"And I can't ever do anything again," she gasped. "I expect I shall never walk again, and no one will ever go on being my friend! Oh, I wish I could die!"

I was feeling really sorry for her now, and I flung my arm around her shoulders.

"I will go on being your friend, Phil," I said in real distress. "Only I must go with the others sometimes. I'm really sorry you can't walk, and I'll come whenever I can. But you mustn't be cross if I don't come some days because soon it will be school, and I shall have homework and things. I promise I'll do my best."

"Don't you like coming to see me?" asked Philippa, turning over and sniffing pathetically.

"Of course I do," I answered, "but I like doing things with Jan, too, sometimes." I was beginning to think that Philippa was rather selfish.

"Oh, I know you like Jan far better than me," replied Philippa, and she disappeared again under the bedcovers. Because I had never been ill myself, and because no one had brought me up to care much about other people, I soon got impatient and went home, saying that I'd come back when she was in a better mood.

The summer term started soon after that, and I was busier than ever. I stopped enjoying Philippa's company very much because she usually spent most of the time grumbling and sulking because I hadn't been there the day before, and we often quarrelled. I had quite forgotten that I, too, had once felt left out and sorry for myself, and because I wasn't used to making myself do things that I didn't like, my visits became fewer and fewer.

"You'd better go today," said Janet rather anxiously one afternoon as we cycled home from school. "She likes you much better than me now."

"I don't see why I should," I answered crossly. "She's so spoiled and selfish. All she does is grumble and ask why I don't come every day. She can't expect me to do nothing but sit with her."

Janet was silent. Then she sighed. "It must be pretty awful," she said thoughtfully, "never being able to run about. I sometimes think, Elaine . . . I wish we could tell her about Jesus. She'd be much happier then. Daddy's talked lots to Mrs. Thomas, but she said that if there really was a God, why did He let this happen to Philippa? So she couldn't be bothered with religion. I heard Daddy telling Mummy about it."

I felt rather uncomfortable because I had thought the same thing. But I knew it was no good trying to tell Philippa about Jesus if I quarrelled with her and got impatient and didn't bother going to see her.

Well, I would have to think about it, but not just then, because we were reaching home and I was hungry. I bounced into the kitchen, where tea was laid, and ate five thick slices of bread and jam and drank four cups of tea. Mrs. Owen laughed at me.

"Elaine," she said as I got up to go, "we'll have to weigh you. You've put on so much weight over the holidays that I don't believe your mother would recognize you. I think you'll have to stay with us forever."

I smiled at her and skipped out the door, feeling strong and alive and happy. Yes, Mrs. Owen was right—the country suited me, and I never, never wanted to go back to London. I would like to see Mummy again, but she could come and visit me here.

I arrived all rosy and breathless at Philippa's window and came down to earth with a bump at the sight of her pale, cross little face. A delicious tea with a plate of iced cakes lay untasted beside her. I sat with my back to them because they made my mouth water.

"Why didn't you come yesterday?" began Philippa as usual. "I waited for you all evening."

"Too much homework," I answered shortly. "And I can't stay long tonight. We only got in from school at half-past four; we were late coming up from games. Do you know, Philippa, we've started playing tennis. It's great fun!"

"I wish I could play tennis," sighed Philippa, "or even go to school! It's really boring always doing lessons alone. I've been trying today, but it's no fun. Tell me what lessons you do, Elaine. I wonder if they are the same as mine."

For once she seemed willing to listen to me instead of talking about her troubles. We were getting on much better than usual, and I wondered if I could possibly tell her about the Bible and Jesus.

"What lessons do you like best?" she asked.

"Well," I answered rather hesitantly, "what I like best isn't a school lesson at all. It's a sort of lesson Jan and I do together before breakfast. We read the Bible together and choose a verse for the day and write it down, and it sort of helps us all day. Do you ever read the Bible, Phil?"

She shook her head but looked at me rather curiously. "Mrs. Owen once talked to me about it and gave me a book of Bible stories," she said, "but

100

Mummy says the Bible isn't suitable for children, and I used to think it was really boring when we read it at school prayers. Do you really like it, Elaine?"

I nodded. "I used to be like you," I said, "and my mum never told me anything about it. I thought it was just a big, black, dull book full of long words, until I came to the Owens'. But then, one day, something happened to me."

"What?" asked Philippa, her blue eyes very big and serious.

"Well," I answered slowly, not quite knowing how to explain, "I did something very wrong, and I was all miserable and frightened, and I ran away into a wood. Mr. Owen came to look for me, and we stayed talking in the wood for ages. He told me that if I told Jesus about the wrong things I'd done, He would forgive me, and after that I'd always belong to Him."

"And what happened then?" asked Philippa.

"Well," I answered slowly, "I did it, and now I do belong to Him."

"And what difference does it make?" asked Philippa. There seemed to be an almost mocking look in her big blue eyes that I couldn't quite understand.

"Well," I said hesitatingly, "I've been ever so much happier since. You see, if you belong to Jesus, it's like having a friend you can tell things to. I don't get all miserable and frightened like I used to. You sort of feel safe."

"And what else?" Philippa went on. "Is that all?"

"Well, it's quite a lot," I answered rather crossly,

"but of course there are other things as well. Jesus teaches you to be good."

"And are you good?" demanded Philippa.

"I'm better than I used to be," I replied. "I was always getting angry and losing my temper and being horrid, and now I don't—at least, not so much."

"Oh," said Philippa in a voice I didn't like at all.

I glanced at the clock. "I must go!" I cried, jumping to my feet. "I'll never finish my homework. Shall I bring you my Bible the next time, Phil? Then you can see for yourself."

"All right," said Philippa rather coldly. "You can bring it if you like. I want you to come to tea the day after tomorrow—Saturday. Will you promise to come, Elaine?"

I was halfway through the door in a hurry to be off. "OK," I answered. "I expect I can come. I'll do my best."

"No, no," shouted Philippa. "You've got to promise. It's very special this time. You will come, won't you?"

"Yes, all right," I called back rather impatiently, because Philippa often said things were special when I couldn't see anything special about them. "I said I'd come, so don't worry."

As I ran down the hill, Philippa's words rang in my ears, although I didn't want to think about them. "What difference does it make? Are you good?"

I was certainly happier, but was I really nicer? Or was it just Peter and Janet were much nicer to me? What was I like with selfish, spoiled people? What was I like with weak, ill people? Was I really patient and kind? And why had Philippa looked at me like that?

"Jan," I said that night, "do you remember that part your dad showed you in the Bible the night I ran away? Something about hungry people and ill people?"

"Yes," said Janet, "I underlined it in red; it was in Matthew 25. I was going to show it to you, but I forgot."

She found the verses and read them slowly, and I listened to them all, but certain words stayed specially in my mind: "I was . . . sick . . . and you did not visit Me. . . . Inasmuch as you did not do it to one of the least of these, you did not do it to Me."

14

A Birthday Remembered

Saturday was another beautiful day, and as we gathered around the dinner table, Janet suddenly looked out of the open window and said, "Mum, could we take tea to the river and swim this afternoon?"

A joyful roar greeted this suggestion, for we had not been swimming that year. Mrs. Owen glanced rather doubtfully outside, but the still-golden sunshine reassured her, and she agreed it would be a very good idea.

"Come with us, Daddy," coaxed Johnny, climbing onto his father's knee. "You said you'd teach me to swim."

Mr. Owen was a very busy man, and his company was a rare treat, but he shook his head sadly. "Got to get into my best black suit and marry someone," he said with a sigh. He looked out to the sparkling blue sea in the distance. "Fancy wanting to get married on an afternoon like this when you could be splashing in the river!"

"Never mind, Dad," comforted Peter. "You'll get a lovely tea."

"Maybe," said his father, "but I'd rather eat buns in the mud with you. Never mind! I'll keep next Saturday free and take you all to the beach—mums, babies, prams, dogs, and all!"

He scattered the children and went off to get ready, and we rushed in all directions collecting fishing rods, sandwiches, lemonade, Cadwaller, and towels.

Mrs. Owen was rather worried about Francie going, too, but Peter promised to look after her really well.

"The river's so shallow, we couldn't drown her if we wanted to," he said.

"Which we don't," added Johnny.

"Remember, Francie is very small. Dry her properly, Janet," said Mrs. Owen. "And don't sit around in wet swimming things. And Elaine, don't stay in too long, and don't forget—"

"No, Mummy. Yes, Mummy. We won't forget anything, we promise," we shouted, all kissing her good-bye at once and dashing off up the hill. The countryside, bathed in sunshine, was beautiful. We all went mad and pushed one another around and laughed over nothing at all till we couldn't stop, as happy children will when spring has got into their blood.

When we reached the top of the valley where we could see the river below, I suddenly remembered something and stood stock-still.

"Whatever's the matter?" asked Janet, turning around to see why I'd stopped. "Have you swallowed a fly?"

"I've just remembered," I answered slowly, "I promised I'd go to tea with Philippa."

There was a long, dismayed silence. Then Janet spoke.

"You'd better go back," she said flatly. "Or . . . I suppose I could go back instead. I mean, if it was a promise, I suppose someone had better keep it."

"Come on, you girls," shouted Peter. He had reached the bank and had already changed into his swimming trunks. Johnny and Frances were struggling with their buttons.

I stood thinking deeply. I had said I'd go back and take the Bible. If I failed, she'd never believe that the Bible made any difference to anyone. I stared again at the inviting little path, and it reminded me of my special verse: "You will show me the path of life; in Your presence is fullness of joy." And suddenly I knew very clearly what path He was showing me that afternoon—not the one that led down to the cool river, but the one that led back over the fields to Philippa— the path of unselfishness and kindness and keeping one's promises. That was where I would find Jesus.

I drew a long breath and turned back. "I'd better go," I said. "Good-bye. Have a nice time."

"Good-bye," answered Janet, much relieved. "We'll come again another time—there'll be lots more chances to swim." She rushed off down the valley, unfastening her dress as she ran.

It seemed a long, hot walk home, and I tried hard not to think of the others splashing in the river. Yet I was not really as unhappy as I thought I would be. I think it was the first time in my life I had given up doing something I really wanted to do for the sake of someone else, and it was a strange, rather pleasant feeling. I reached the house at last and retrieved my Bible. When I reached Philippa's house it was half past four, and Mrs. Thomas was standing at the gate looking rather anxious.

"Oh, Elaine," she said in a relieved voice, "I'm so glad you've come. You see, it's Philippa's birthday, and I was going to have a party, but she wanted you all by yourself, and she said you'd promised to come. She was getting in such a state, thinking you'd forgotten."

She led me into the garden, where Philippa lay in a deck chair by the rockery with tea spread out beside her, and a beautiful pink birthday cake with ten candles. She looked very pretty in a new blue summer dress she had received as a present, and I, hot and crumpled, in my oldest clothes and muddy shoes, felt rather ashamed of myself.

"Where have you been?" asked Philippa. "I thought you'd forgotten. You didn't know it was my birthday, did you?"

"No," I answered, "or I'd have brought you a present. Happy birthday, Philippa! I'm sorry I'm late, but the others went swimming in the river, and I went some of the way with them and then came back by myself."

"Oh," said Philippa, looking at me curiously, "and

why did you do that? Did you forget you were coming to tea with me?"

"Well, yes," I replied truthfully, "I did at first, because Pete thought of swimming only at dinner-time, suddenly, and we all got rather excited. But as soon as I remembered, I came back quick."

"Oh, I see," said Philippa. Then she added, "Do you like swimming?"

"Yes, I do," I answered. "But it doesn't matter. Mr. Owen's going to take us to the sea next week. We're not allowed to swim alone in the sea, but the river's shallow. Even Francie went."

Then Mrs. Thomas arrived with the teapot, and we had a very happy tea party. Mrs. Thomas told us funny stories, and I stuffed myself with cakes and cookies and sandwiches. Then we lit the candles, which didn't show at all in the sunshine, and Philippa cut the cake.

When I could eat no more, Mrs. Thomas picked up the tray. "I'm going to wash up the tea things now," she said, "and leave you two together. Philippa, do you want to show Elaine your presents?"

"Later," said Philippa. "We'll stay here for a bit now, because we've got a secret." She waited till her mother had disappeared, and then she turned to me eagerly. "Have you brought your Bible, Elaine?" she asked.

"Yes," I answered, rather surprised, for she had not seemed particularly interested before. "It's here under my chair. I'll show it to you."

"It's like this," said Philippa. "I've been thinking. You said that when you know Jesus, it makes you good, and I think I'll believe you now, because you came back from swimming when I know you wanted to go. If you hadn't come back, I'd have thought it was all silly pretending. And you said it was like having a friend you could tell things to, and I just wondered—if I read my Bible and prayed, do you think Jesus would make me walk again?"

I hesitated. "He *could* make you walk again," I said simply. "He did heal people lots of times. He was always making people better. Mark's Gospel is full of stories about people who were ill and got healed."

"Well, read me one," commanded Philippa.

"I'll read what I read this morning," I said confidently. "It was about a man who couldn't walk at all, so his friends let him down through a hole in the roof, and first of all Jesus said, 'Your sins are forgiven,' and then He made him walk. Here it is, I've found it." I read her the story of the paralyzed man in Mark 2, and she listened intently, her eyes fixed on my face.

"It said in the notes," I remarked thoughtfully, "that the most important thing is to have your sins forgiven. Then you can start asking for other things."

Philippa frowned. "I don't think I've got an awful lot of sins," she said. "How could I, lying here? I couldn't really be very naughty if I tried."

"You can be bad-tempered," I answered, "and you do grumble a lot. I think that counts as sin. I used to get terribly cross before I loved Jesus."

"You still are, sometimes," retorted Philippa. "But never mind, let's not quarrel today. Tell me how you get your sins forgiven."

"You just ask," I said simply, "and you believe that Jesus died for you. That's all, I think."

Philippa shook her head. "I don't believe it's as easy as all that," she said firmly. "Let's not bother about sins. Let's just ask Jesus to make me walk. Do you know how, Elaine?"

I looked doubtful. "I don't think you can do it like that, Philippa," I answered. "I'm sure you've got to belong to Jesus first. Let me ask Mrs. Owen about it, and then I'll come and tell you."

"All right," said Philippa, "you ask her. I don't believe you know an awful lot about it yourself, Elaine. Now come and see my presents."

I helped her indoors and admired her beautiful gifts, and then I said good-bye and thank you to Mrs. Thomas and went trotting home. To my surprise, the others had not returned. It was one of those very rare occasions when I could have Mrs. Owen all to myself. She was in the kitchen, ironing.

"Auntie," I said, "I want to ask you something very important. Can you pray for things before you've had your sins forgiven?"

She looked up, startled. "Why have you come home, Elaine?" She asked. "Where are the others?"

"I forgot I promised to go to tea with Philippa," I explained, "so I came back . . . and Philippa wants to know. She wants me to pray that she'll get better, but she doesn't want to bother about having her sins forgiven. She says she hasn't got many."

Mrs. Owen switched off her iron and gave me her whole attention. I discovered later that she prayed each day for Philippa and her mother.

"It tells us in the Bible that God is so pure and holy that we can't come to Him at all until we've been made clean and forgiven by the Lord Jesus," she answered.

Our peace was shattered as the back door was flung open and the children burst into the kitchen, sunburned, messy, and noisy, trailing wet swimming things, with Cadwaller covered in mud leaping behind them.

"Mum," announced Peter, "there were some Boy Scouts in tents by the river, camping. Mum, please, can we all go camping?"

Mrs. Owen blinked, as she always did when switched too suddenly from one subject to another. "Why, yes, Peter," she answered, "I think it would be lovely. But you didn't mean tonight, did you?"

"No, Mum, not tonight," said Peter. "We would need weeks and weeks to get ready. I mean in the summer holidays. You said we couldn't afford to go somewhere together, but camping wouldn't cost anything at all. We'd go to the mountains, and we'd go on bikes, and you and the babies and everything else could come on the bus. We'd go on Dad's holiday, and he'd take us up Snowdon."

"Who's taking me up Snowdon?" asked the vicar, coming in at that moment and flinging himself down rather wearily into the old kitchen chair, and holding out his arms to Frances, who leaped joyfully into his lap.

"Mum says we can go camping in the mountains this summer," said Peter eagerly. "You said you'd take us climbing this year, didn't you, Dad?"

111

"Why, yes," agreed Mr. Owen, as eager as Peter. "I've been waiting for years for you to be old enough to start on the big mountains, and I'd have taken you all last August, only you spoiled it by having chicken pox. It will be extra good fun this year, because we will have Elaine with us. We need to find a farmhouse for Mum and the little ones, and one tent for me and Pete and Johnny and one for the girls."

"Me in the tent," whispered Frances. "Oh, say I can be in the tent!"

"Of course," answered Mr. Owen, laughing. "I'm not sleeping out in the wilds of Snowdon without Francie to look after me!" And he drew her smooth, mousy head against his shoulder and gave her a hug.

15

A Sudden Meeting

I was so eager to finish my conversation with Mrs. Owen that as soon as our lights were out that night I slipped out of bed and crept downstairs in my night clothes. She was sitting alone in the living room, so I sat down on the rug and went on where I'd left off.

"It's funny Philippa doesn't think she's got any sins," I began, "because she's really awfully selfish and cross. Couldn't you come and explain it to her, Auntie?"

She was silent for a moment, and then, instead of answering me, she said, "I'll tell you a story, and you try to think what it means.

"There was once an old woman who lived in a little village in the mountains, and one day in winter she went to town and bought a packet of washing powder that was supposed to be very good. She did her laundry and hung it out to dry, and it certainly did look whiter than the clothes in the other cottage gardens. She was so pleased that she left it out for two whole days so that everyone could see it. Then it became bitterly cold, and she thought, 'I must bring in my washing before nighttime.' So out she went, but when she got into the garden, she threw up her hands in horror and said, 'Who's been meddling with my washing? It's not white anymore—in fact, it looks almost gray.'

"No one had meddled with her washing, and in a moment or two she realized what had happened. While she was busy indoors, the snow had fallen on the mountains. And against that pure dazzling whiteness—God's whiteness—her laundered clothes seemed gray."

She glanced at me, smiling, but I was frowning in a puzzled way, not quite understanding.

"Lots of people are like that old woman," said Mrs. Owen. "They look at their neighbors and say, 'I'm not a sinner, I'm better than So-and so, and I'm much less selfish than So-and-so.' And they quite forget that God never tells them to be like So-and-so. He says, 'Be holy, for I am holy,'* and He sent Jesus to show us just how perfect and holy He is. It's when we look at Jesus in the Bible that we see God's perfect, shining whiteness, perfect courage, perfect goodness, and perfect love. And the more we look, the more we realise, 'I am not like that.'"

*1 Peter 1:16

"I see," I answered slowly. "I've got to keep telling Philippa about Jesus, and when she sees what He's like, she'll see what she's like, and till then, I suppose she mustn't ask to be made better."

Mrs. Owen shook her head, smiling.

"Lots of people came to Jesus in the Bible who only thought about getting better," she said simply. "He was so kind and loving that He always said 'Come.' He never turned anyone away. He just gave them more than they asked for. He let them see His face and hear His voice, and I expect that was far more wonderful to them than being healed. You let Philippa pray any way she likes; Jesus Himself will teach her if she really means what she is saying. You've got just three things to do."

"What?" I asked.

"First, pray for her, and we all will, too. Then make special times to go and visit her and read the Bible together, and stick to them faithfully. Lastly, show her the love and care and patience of Jesus in your own life. If He is really living in your heart, she ought to be able to see Him in you, not only in the Bible."

I sat thinking silently, and a few moments later Mr. Owen came in, and we told him what we had been talking about. He was very interested and asked whether Philippa had a Bible of her own.

"No," I answered, "but I could buy her one for a birthday present. What would it cost?"

"A nicely printed one would cost quite a lot," said Mr. Owen, "but I think Janet would like to help. Tell her about it in the morning, and you could go into town together and choose it."

I went up to bed feeling very happy, and the next morning I told Janet about my plan. She was delighted and promised to give every penny she had, but that was not much, because she was an extremely generous little girl and was always giving presents.

We were spreading our joint collection on the table to count it properly when Peter came in.

"What are you doing with all that money?" he asked suspiciously. "Don't forget; we've got to save for camp. I'm going to try to buy a map and a compass, so you'll have to help with other things."

"But it's for Philippa's Bible," explained Janet, "and I think it's more important than camp. Elaine has started telling her about Jesus."

"Oh, I see," said Peter, scratching his head thoughtfully. He was a very shy boy in some ways and never talked about his deepest thoughts.

"Well, you don't seem to have much between you," he said suddenly, and marched out of the room.

"Oh, dear!" said Janet, who adored her brother. "I'm afraid he's cross. After all, we did say we'd save for camp, but I thought there was still time for that. We've got all our pocket money for two months, and we can do some odd jobs."

She was interrupted by Peter's clattering feet. He marched into the room and threw some coins on the table.

"Might as well get her a decent one while you're about it," he said gruffly. "And when you go to choose it, I'll come with you." He was gone before we could even say "Thank you," slamming the door

116

very hard behind him.

We set off early the next morning on our bicycles, since the nearest town where Bibles could be bought was seven miles away. We went the back way through winding roads to avoid the traffic.

It was Whitsun holiday, and the town was very busy and crowded with holidaymakers. At last we found the bookshop, and a kind shop girl asked us which Bible we wanted.

"We'd like to see them all, please," said Peter grandly, "as long as they don't cost too much."

The girl smiled and waited patiently. For ten minutes we looked and argued and discussed and changed our minds. But in the end we all agreed on a beautiful clothbound one with large print and pictures.

"Good," said Peter with a sigh of relief. "Now, let's have one ice cream each, and that still leaves a bit for camp. Come on!"

We were standing in a doorway eating our ice cream when I suddenly saw him, and my heart seemed to miss a beat. I looked again. Yes, it was definitely the face that had haunted me for weeks— an ugly, unshaven face with wild, frightened eyes.

"Peter," I whispered, clutching hold of him so hard he dropped his ice cream. "Peter, it's him!"

"Who?" retorted Peter. "Look out, Elaine!"

"Never mind your ice cream, Peter," I breathed urgently. "Look, *look!* There by the crossing! It's the man I saw in the Thomases' garden! Oh, Peter, let's get away quick. He may see me!"

I cowered down in a doorway, but I was too late.

At a sign from a policeman, a crowd swarmed across the road, leaving a gap. The man turned suddenly and recognized me. The next instant he dived off into the crowds and disappeared up a side street.

"Quick!" shouted Peter. "There's a policeman—tell him!"

He plunged toward the policeman. "We've seen the thief who took the things from Mrs. Thomas's house," he yelled, clutching hold of his sleeve. "He's just run off, but I'm sure you could catch him if you tried."

The policeman shook him off impatiently. "I don't care if you've seen the thief who robbed Buckingham Palace," he retorted, his eyes on the traffic. "I've got my job to do. If you have anything to report, you can go to the police station up Emrys Street."

"It's no good," said Peter disappointedly. "It would take us half an hour to get to Emrys Street in these crowds, and he could have gone anywhere by then. There are buses leaving all the time. Oh, to think I got as near as that and missed him!"

We moved into a side street and leaned miserably against the wall.

"I don't think the police take much notice of children, anyhow," Peter went on. "We'd better get home quickly and tell Dad. He could always phone if he liked. Anyhow, one good thing—I've seen him myself now, and I would know him again anywhere!"

16

The Child at the Door

The summer sped by and, without knowing it, I was changing—growing taller and more sturdy. I had also really started to enjoy school and was beginning to realize what a beautiful world I lived in. It was as though my eyes had been opened.

I was learning other lessons too. Three times a week, I climbed the hill in the light of the evenings after supper and sat for half an hour with Philippa. Sometimes Janet came, too, and we always spent part of that time reading the Bible. Philippa's Bible had become her dearest possession. All through her illness, she had had nothing much to think about but herself, and she was tired and bored and unhappy. Even her storybooks bothered her because they were mostly about strong, healthy children who ran about and had adventures. But the Bible opened up a wonderful new world to her. It was all about sick children who were healed, sad people who were comforted, tired people who found rest, lost sheep that were found, and sinful people who were forgiven. In the midst of them all was Jesus, who called them to come to Him, and in whose presence was fullness of joy.

"I do love Him," said Philippa suddenly one night. "I wish I really belonged to Him, like you. But He hasn't made me walk yet, and I sometimes wonder if He really listens to me."

"You could belong to Him like I do," I said simply, "but when I tell you how, you never seem to understand. I'm going to ask Mrs. Owen to come. She'll tell you. She's ever so good at explaining things. I'll bring her before we go camping."

Philippa's face brightened. "Yes, do," she answered. "I like Mrs. Owen. I'd like to make certain before you go camping, because I won't see you for a whole ten days. Still, Daddy's coming home after that, so that's something to look forward to."

Plans for camping had been going well, and it was all we could think and talk about. By the time I reached the garden gate, I knew that something very exciting had happened, for I could hear the noise quite a long way away. I dashed up the path to find out what it was all about. "What's happened?" I shouted. "Tell me quickly!"

"A car for the holiday!" yelled Peter. "Mr. Jones is so grateful to Dad for making Mrs. Jones better that he's lending him his car for August. We will be able to explore everywhere now, and Mum and the little ones will be able to come too."

"Steady, Pete," broke in Mr. Owen. "I'm not a doctor."

But we all knew about poor Mrs. Jones, whose first baby had died quite suddenly. The doctor could do nothing to help her, and it was only Mr. Owen's prayers and patient daily visits that saved her from going crazy. She was now up and about again, visiting others who were sad. No wonder Mr. Jones was grateful.

Having a car was really wonderful news, for there weren't many mountain buses, and Lucy seemed to need so much luggage. Now we could take the camping equipment in advance, and then come back for Mrs. Owen and the younger ones. Besides, we could reach the foot of the great mountains by car, do some real climbing in the day, and get back to camp at night. Peter had even produced a climbing rope.

We were to leave on the second day of the summer holiday. Mrs. Owen was very busy preparing everything, so I waited till Sunday to ask her about Philippa. She said she would go to see Philippa right after supper, so that evening we set out together. When we reached the grassy slope under the old beech trees, Mrs. Owen stopped and sat down on the mossy roots.

"Let's pray before we go in," she said. I sat down beside her and closed my eyes, and she asked God to show Philippa the way to Him.

Mrs. Thomas chatted to Mrs. Owen for a few minutes, and then she went off to get the supper and we were left alone.

Philippa turned eagerly to Mrs. Owen. "Good," she said, "you've come! I've been waiting every day. Did Elaine tell you?"

"Yes," answered Mrs. Owen. "You are worried, aren't you, because you've asked God to make you walk properly, and He hasn't, and you can't understand why?"

Philippa nodded. Her eyes were fixed on Mrs. Owen's face as though she was listening to some wonderful secret.

"I think it's like this," said Mrs. Owen, speaking very slowly. "Supposing a ragged, homeless boy came to my door and asked me for fifty pence. I could give him fifty pence and send him away, or I could do something far better. I could say to him, 'I'm not going to give you fifty pence, but I'm going to take you into my home and love you and wash you clean and care for you, and make you my own little child.' If I said that, do you think that little boy would go on worrying about his fifty pence? He'd know that I loved him enough to give him every single thing he needed."

"Is the fifty pence like my legs?" asked Philippa. She was a very quick child in some ways.

"A little bit," answered Mrs. Owen. "You've asked the Lord Jesus to give you strong legs, and He's looking down at you and saying, 'Philippa, I've got something far better for you than that. I love you, and I want you to be My own little girl. I want to save you from all your crossness and sadness and selfishness, and I want to make you happy.' Of course, later on He may give you strong legs as well, and you can go on asking Him. But first of all He wants to teach you that if you belong to Him, you can be happy even lying here on this couch. Has Elaine shown you the verse written in the front of her Bible?"

"Yes," answered Philippa at once. "I can say it: 'You will show me the path of life; in Your presence is fullness of joy.'"

"Good," said Mrs. Owen. "It means that when we come to the Lord Jesus, we tell Him that we are willing for Him to choose our path of life, because He knows best. And that means that even if we have illness or sorrow or disappointments, we will know that He is close beside us. You know, Philippa, happiness doesn't really depend on what you've got or where you are. Real, true, lasting happiness comes from living close to the Lord Jesus and being like Him."

Philippa said nothing. She often turned things over for a long time in her mind before coming to any decisions. A few minutes later Mrs. Thomas came back and begged us to stay for supper.

"I really must get back and see what the family is doing," Mrs. Owen said. "They are all wild with excitement because Mr. Jones has offered to lend my husband a car so we can all go camping. The Joneses are staying with his parents, and they've got a car already, so they were just going to leave theirs in the garage. Isn't it wonderful! I can't tell you how I was dreading carting all the camp gear and little ones on the bus and dragging them miles up a mountain at the other end."

I glanced at Philippa. There was a lonely, wistful little look on her face that filled me with pity. I suddenly had a marvelous idea.

"Auntie," I shouted, "it's not very far with a car! Couldn't Uncle come one day and bring Mrs. Thomas and Philippa to see the camp and come and have tea with us? Oh, Auntie, do say yes!"

Philippa's face had gone pink with excitement, and her eyes were shining. Both mothers looked quite alarmed for a moment.

"We'd have to ask my husband," said Mrs. Owen. "As a matter of fact, if you don't think it's too tiring for Philippa, I would say it was a wonderful idea."

"So would I," said Philippa quickly. "Mummy, if you say yes, I'll never be naughty again!"

We all burst out laughing at this, and then Mrs. Owen and I hurried home through the dark. It was high time, too, for things had not gone too success-fully during her absence. She had the chaotic situa-tion under control in a few moments, then put the kettle on for a cup of tea.

"I should go to see Philippa tomorrow," she remarked peacefully when we were all sitting around the kitchen table. "Now, here come Daddy and Pete. Let's have tea."

It was a pleasant evening, and everyone agreed with my plan of bringing Philippa and her mum to the camp for the day. We could have gone on eating buns and chatting all night if Mrs. Owen hadn't chased us up to bed.

Before lying down, I stood at the open window a few minutes and leaned far out. The warm summer darkness smelled of lavender, and an owl hooted softly from the beech trees. In Philippa's house a light was still burning, and I wondered what she was doing. Was she still standing outside, like the beggar boy asking for gifts, or had she gone in through the door to the light and safety of Jesus' home?

17

The Camp by the Lake

The great morning dawned at last. Mr. Owen set out with us four older children and the tents at the crack of dawn to pitch camp. It was a perfect morning, and we traveled by the narrow back lanes, singing for miles. The dew still lay on the fields when we started, and the spiders' webs shone like silver.

We left the lanes after a time and joined a winding road and began to climb toward the horizon. Suddenly we reached the top of the hill, and Mr. Owen stopped the car abruptly and said, "Look!"

I gave a little gasp, for I had never seen the great mountains so close. Now they stretched out in front of us as far as the eye could see. Peter jumped up and reeled off the names of the proud rocky summits. We knew that hidden away in the valleys were the lakes.

Peter leapt back into the car and prodded his father in the back. "Go on, Dad," he shouted. "Let's get there!"

So we raced down the hill and through the last little town, over an old stone bridge designed by a famous architect called Inigo Jones, and then we left civilization behind us and were speeding toward the steep mountain rising ahead of us. Ten minutes later, we left the last proper road and turned up a steep, stony path that climbed through larch woods, with a stream foaming down over mossy boulders on our right.

"Will the car really go up there?" asked Janet, clutching the back of the seat nervously. "And what will we do if we meet another car?"

"It would be just too bad!" replied Mr. Owen, pulling down into bottom gear and hooting his horn in warning as we twisted around the corners.

We were breathless with excitement, for we knew that in a few minutes we would see the spot that Peter had described to us. We bumped around the corner and there in front of us, clear as green glass, with the shadows of the hills reflected in it, lay the lake.

Mr. Owen stopped the car, and once again we were silent for a moment. I thought I had never seen anything so beautiful. It was so still and so long. Now and then a gull dipped and ruffled the surface with its wings, but otherwise I couldn't see a ripple. I felt as though I had reached an enchanted country where everything seemed to have fallen asleep.

"Oh, Daddy, let's swim," squealed Johnny. "Look, there's a little beach! Couldn't we make camp there?"

"No," replied Mr. Owen. "We've got to get to the other end of the farmhouse. Look, there's a little white road along the edge of the lake. We'll get the tents up and camp fixed, and then we'll have a swim before dinner. We won't bother about cooking today—just corned beef and bread and butter and plums and lemonade; then I can get back early for Mum."

We drove along the little track by the edge of the water, and very soon we caught sight of Mrs. Davies's farm.

There was a sheepfold and a cowshed to one side of it, and a wire run for chickens, and a spring of clear water splashing into a stone trough in front of the door. Mrs. Davies heard us coming and ran out to meet us. She was a neat, dark little woman with rosy cheeks and bright black eyes, with a little girl clinging to her apron and a large sheepdog jumping around her.

"A little friend for Francie," said Mr. Owen, waving at the child.

"And a little friend for Cadwaller," said Johnny, whistling at the sheepdog.

We tumbled out of the car, and Mr. Owen greeted them in Welsh. Mrs. Davies pointed out the driest spot for the campsite and helped us carry our things. We set to work in earnest, laying the groundsheets and hammering in the tent pegs. Then we went to Mrs. Davies, and she took us around to the barn so we could stuff our mattresses with straw. In the corner was a tiny black-and-white calf, very weak and wobbly, peering out from behind its mother.

We carried big stones up from the lake and built the camp fireplace. We stored our firewood in the barn so it would keep dry.

"We'll build an enormous campfire to welcome Mum tonight," said Peter. "We'll all collect wood while Dad goes to get her. Now, come on, let's have a swim before dinner."

We changed in two minutes and raced barefoot over the springy grass to the pebbly stretch of mud that Johnny had already christened "the bathing beach." After our swim we had dinner, then Mr. Owen glanced at his watch and jumped up.

"I must go to get Mum," he said, "and we won't be back till about five o'clock. You can collect firewood and explore around, but don't get lost and, remember, no one is to go near the lake or light a fire until we get back."

He jumped in the car and went bumping off along the lakeside track. It was rather exciting being left on our own.

"You girls wash up," said Peter, "and then let's build an enormous bonfire for tonight. Then let's go to the other end of the lake and follow the stream and see where it goes. It says on my map that there's another big lake over on the other side of the mountain with a steam flowing down that joins this one."

We tidied up and dug a deep hole for our rubbish, and then scattered to collect firewood. I had never been in such wild, rolling scenery with not a living creature to be seen anywhere.

"Come on," shouted Peter's voice from the camp far below me. "You've got hardly any wood, and we want to start soon."

We collected a big pile between us, then started along the edge of the lake, feeling like a party of explorers setting out to discover unknown territory. Peter carried the map and the compass in a leather bag over his shoulder. It was cool and very silent everywhere.

We reached the end of the lake where it narrowed into a rushing white stream. We had our shoes off in a minute and scrambled down the steep banks, then we slipped on the wet stones and went splashing up to our knees in a foaming pool.

"The trees end just ahead," called Peter. "We're coming out onto a rocky, stony sort of place. Let's come out into the open and have a look around, and then we'll go back."

We waded on and found ourselves in a very desolate place indeed. It must have been an old stone quarry once, for piles of broken stones rose up around us, and just in front were the blackened walls of an old, roofless stone building.

"Looks as though it has been burned," said Peter thoughtfully. "Give me a leg up, someone, and let's see inside."

"I think we ought to go home. We mustn't be late for Mum," said Janet firmly. "I don't like that house, Pete. In fact, I don't like this place at all. It's sort of spooky."

I looked around and shivered a little. The piles of stones hid the countryside, and the air was full of the sound of angry, rushing water.

Peter was wading through the mass of weeds that

surrounded the ruin and had pulled himself up on the sill. "I say," he called back excitedly, "it's got all sorts of rooms in it, and someone has made a camp-fire—there are black stones and ashes and an old saucepan. One room is still roofed over, and the window's stuffed with rags. I think someone lives here. I'm going to try the door!"

He jumped down into the nettles, scratching his legs badly, and picked his way down to the door. It was jammed and stuck, but Peter ran at it with his shoulder, and it burst open so suddenly that he fell forward. He got up quickly and backed out, rather frightened, and stood hesitating.

"Shall I go in?" he asked. "Supposing there's some-one there?"

"I would think he'd have come out by now," said Johnny rather sensibly. Then he hopped over the net-tles and stood in the doorway. "I'll go in," he said brightly. "I'm not frightened."

He skipped into the ruin, poking his inquisitive lit-tle nose into one derelict room after another. Then he came tiptoeing back, his eyes round with excite-ment. "Someone does live here," he whispered. "There's a mattress with nice blankets, and some plates and cups, and a box and an old rug on the floor."

"Oh, Peter," I whispered, "let's go home! Supposing they come. They'll be really cross if they find us in their house, and we will never hear them till they are right on top of us, the stream's making such a noise."

"Well, I'd just like to have a quick look," said

Peter uncertainly. "Johnny, you climb on that stone heap and keep a lookout."

Nimble little Johnny was up in a moment and down again as quickly. "There's a man coming up beside the stream," he squeaked, "and he's got a sack over his back and a dead rabbit in his hand! Come on, everybody, run!" And he was away into the tunnel of trees, leaping from boulder to boulder with Peter and Janet just behind him, and me slipping and stumbling and splashing along last of all. On we went, breathless and wet, with bruised, cold feet and aching legs. We didn't feel safe till we reached the quiet hills and the gray levels of the lake.

"There's the car!" shouted Janet, waving her shoes wildly above her head, and the next moment we were all racing along barefoot beside it, with the joyful faces of Frances, Robin, Lucy, and Cadwaller filling the windows and Mrs. Owen calling out greetings. And although none of us would have confessed it, never before in our lives had we been so pleased to see them.

18

Philippa's Day

The sun seemed to come out as Mrs. Owen struggled out of the car, her arms full of Lucy and a bursting bag of homemade buns. We all flung ourselves upon her, and the rest of the evening was a great success. Mr. Owen had the fire going and the kettles boiling in no time, and we sat around, warming our chilly legs and drying our wet skirts and trousers. Soon we were all eating buns and drinking mugs of hot, sweet tea that tasted of wood smoke and condensed milk, and discussing what we should have for supper.

"I think we'll have eggs and bacon tonight as a treat," said Mrs. Owen, "and finish up with hot chocolate and cookies around the campfire. Perhaps Mrs. Davies and her little girl will join us. Now, let's unpack the food and—oh, Elaine, I almost forgot! There's a letter for you from your mother."

She handed me a thin letter with a French stamp on it, and a funny little cold feeling of fear seemed to rise up inside me, for Mummy hardly ever wrote letters. She sent me postcards every week or so, but they didn't say very much. I turned away from the others and ran up the hill to where I'd gathered firewood, and sat down on the roots of a larch tree, crumpling the letter in my hand. It was silly to feel afraid, for the last time she'd written she'd sent three pounds for camp.

I tore the letter open and read it through several times, because at first I really could not take it in, and yet I'd known all along that it must come one day. The man Mummy worked for was coming home in the autumn. She would keep her job, but she would find a home for us both in London. "You'd better stay and finish your school term," she wrote, "but you will be back with me for the Christmas holidays, and we'll find a school in London after that. I've missed you so much, and it will be lovely to be together again."

The Christmas holidays! Janet had told me all about them: the frosty evenings when they sang carols and left little gifts all around the village by lantern light; the tobogganing and the opening of stockings on Christmas morning; the Sunday school party in the fellowship hall, when Mr. Owen dressed up as Father Christmas —and now I would miss it all.

I gazed down at the campsite. Peter and Johnny were dragging an enormous log up from the barn, and

Janet was leaning over a saucepan, cooking something. Frances stood alone on the little beach with her back to everyone. No! I could not leave them. They were my brothers and sisters now. Surely Mrs. Owen would understand and help me explain to Mummy. Of course, I wanted to see her and I would not mind going to London sometimes, but she could come and visit me in Wales. My home was here in the country now, with the Owen family.

I thought about the last few months. How miserable and selfish I'd been at first, and how I'd hated it! Yet somehow I'd been drawn in. What was it, I wondered, that bound us together and made us such a strong family circle? I was beginning to realize even then that the center of that home was the open Bible —that old, wise Book that taught children to honor and obey their parents, and to love one another, and to recognize life's true values. Who would go on teaching me in London? How could I go on being a Christian all by myself?

"Come on, Elaine," shouted Peter impatiently. "We're going to fry the bacon. Everyone has to sit down with a plate."

A delicious smell came floating up, and I went down to join the family. Mrs. Owen pushed Johnny out of the way and made a place for me, and I snuggled comfortably against her. Perhaps she guessed what was in my letter.

Supper was a great success, and afterward we piled wood on the fire and made a blaze that lit up the dark mountains all around and made rosy reflections on the black lake. Mrs. Davies and her daughter and

135

Tudor, the sheepdog, joined us for hot chocolate and cookies, and we sang campfire songs till we were hoarse. Then Mr. Owen opened his Bible and read to us. As we sat listening, the moon rose over the far end of the valley, flooding the lake with silver light. We slept with our tent flaps thrown back so that the moonbeams could shine down on us all night long.

Every day in camp was so exciting. We swam in the lake before breakfast. Peter was in charge of the fire, and Janet and I were the cooks, with Mrs. Owen giving advice. Sometimes we went on expeditions and climbed the mountains, and sometimes we just explored the near hills or messed around the farm. When the rain and mists came sweeping over the mountains, we played in the barn, and on wet evenings Mrs. Davies made us welcome in her kitchen, which we loved. It had an uneven stone floor and a huge fireplace that took up most of one side of the wall. It was a very cozy place to be on rainy nights when the thunder broke over the mountains. We used to get ready for bed in Mrs. Davies' room and then dash up the dark slope in the storm and dive into our sleeping bags.

One cloudless day, we climbed Snowdon. Another day, with the help of Peter's map, we discovered every lake hidden away in the secret folds of the hills and climbed every rocky peak. I was becoming as brown as a berry and as strong as a mountain pony, and I sometimes wondered what my mother would think of me if she saw me.

But to me the great event of the holiday was Philippa's visit, and on Saturday morning, long before the others were awake, I wriggled out of my sleeping bag and crept to the door of the tent to look at the weather. It was still very early, but the sky behind the mountains was pearly blue, and the morning star was still shining over the highest crag.

It's going to be a beautiful day, I thought to myself, shivering a little. *There isn't a cloud to be seen.* I pulled my blanket around my shoulders and watched the sky grow brighter and brighter behind the rocks. And because I was too excited to feel sleepy, I stayed there watching until at last the sun appeared, and the grass all around me turned to silver and the waters of the lake to gold.

"Oh, wake up, Janet," I said impatiently. "Come and swim! The water's all shiny." But Janet only grunted and disappeared far down into her sleeping bag, leaving me Cadwaller for company.

Everything seemed to move slowly that morning. No one seemed in any hurry except me, and at last I could bear it no longer. I rushed up to Mr. Owen, who was sitting in the sun listening to one of Frances's stories, and asked him what time he was thinking of getting Philippa.

"Philippa?" said Mr. Owen calmly, glancing at his watch. "Why, yes, she was coming out to dinner today, wasn't she? I'd better start now while the weather's fine and get her out early. It could cloud over later."

He got up and glanced at the car. "We'll leave the whole backseat for Philippa," he said, "but there's room for three in the front. Like to come with me, Elaine? It would be fun for Philippa to have you on the way back."

I was thrilled and rushed off to get ready.

It was a lovely drive, and when we arrived we found Philippa had been ready for ages, sitting at the window. Within five minutes we were off again, Philippa stretched out on the backseat, and me sandwiched between Mr. Owen and Mrs. Thomas, leaning over the back to talk to her. Of course, there was an awful lot to tell, and I chattered on without stopping, for Philippa wanted to know every detail of what we'd been doing.

"And what have you been doing?" I asked when we were nearly there.

"Nothing much," answered Philippa, quite cheerfully. "Just sitting!"

I glanced at her in surprise, for she was not speaking in her usual whiny, self-pitying voice. She looked at me straight in the eyes and pursed her lips to whisper. "I want to tell you something when we're alone," she said mysteriously, and I nodded and winked, for I liked secrets.

"Oh," cried Philippa as we turned the corner to the campsite, "there they are, and look, there's a lake. Oh, Elaine, what a beautiful place!"

Mr. Owen put on the brakes rather suddenly, for the five children had come to meet us and were standing with joined hands across the road, sunburned, laughing, and dishevelled. Then, with a whoop of delight, they were off, pelting over the springy turf in an effort to race the car. But Mr. Owen pressed on the accelerator, and in a few moments we'd left them far behind, and Philippa and I stuck our heads out of the window and yelled with triumph.

There was a bed of bracken and heather arranged on the hillside for Philippa, and Mr. Owen carried her up over the rough ground and laid her down gently by the camp. Dinner was almost ready, and it was a real feast for the occasion—sausages, potatoes baked in the ashes then split open and stuffed with butter, and a huge plum pie made by Mrs. Davies.

Feeling very full, we all lay on the ground eating sweets, which Philippa had brought. Mrs. Owen started reading *The Wind in the Willows* to us. She had only finished one chapter when Mrs. Thomas pointed rather anxiously to the far end of the lake. A strange white mist was creeping through a gap in the hills, like a thief with cold hands. The trees were looking dim and ghostly, and a chill seemed to be creeping over the face of the sun.

19

A Shock and a Meeting

I think we should be going home," said Mrs. Thomas. "I don't want Philippa to get cold. It's been such a lovely treat for both of us."

"Oh, Mummy," pleaded Philippa, "just wait five minutes. The mist's coming ever so slowly, and I want to talk to Elaine for a minute. I won't see her for another five whole days."

"Very well, darling," said Mrs. Thomas, "just five minutes. I'm going with Francie and Robin to see the baby calf."

Peter, Janet, and Johnny went off to do the washing up in the lake, and I sprawled on the grass beside Philippa's bracken nest. She was bursting with her secret and came straight to the point.

"Elaine," she began, "do you remember what Mrs.

Owen said about begging at the door or going in?"

"Yes," I answered, "of course I do. Have you gone in, Phil?"

"Yes, I think so," replied Philippa rather shyly. "I thought about it so much. And one night, instead of saying, 'Please make my legs better,' I said, 'Please, can I come inside and be Your own little girl?' And from that day I've had a sort of feeling that I might be happy even if my legs didn't get any better. I've asked Jesus to change me and stop me being selfish and cross, and now I keep having new ideas about what I could do. It's rather fun. I'd never thought of them before because I used to think there was nothing nice to do if you couldn't walk. Only I'm longing for you to come home and help me with them."

"What sort of ideas?" I asked, deeply interested.

"Oh, things like helping Mummy, and making things for people," said Philippa, "and seeing how long I can go without grumbling and making a fuss about my lessons. I haven't time to explain now, but I keep on thinking about your verse. If it was my path of life to be unable to walk, it says I could still be happy, doesn't it?"

"Yes," I said firmly. "Fullness of joy, anywhere, if we are walking the path of life with Jesus. Mr. Owen has explained it to me lots of times."

"Philippa," called Mrs. Thomas, "we really must be going, or we shall be caught in the mist."

The next moment Mr. Owen bounded up the slope and picked Philippa up in his arms. There was just time to show her the calf on the way down, and then she was lifted into the car. A delighted Frances peeped out from between the grown-ups in the middle of the front seat. She was going to drive back alone with her father, and they were going to stop off at a tea shop.

The car set off into the cold, creeping white mist. Peter and I followed as far as the trees at the top of the lane. It was going to be an evening for Mrs. Davies's kitchen and the cozy fireside.

"I've never seen such a thick mist before," said Peter, looking around. "I can't see the lake at all. Look, there's someone coming down that path, Elaine. A man! I wonder where he's going. Not many people come this way."

The man did not see us, but we could see him quite clearly. He had a bag slung over his shoulder that clattered a little, as though he were carrying pots and pans, and the moment I saw him, I knew him. A chill ran through me that had nothing to do with the mist. Peter stood rigid and uncertain beside me; he, too, had caught a glimpse of that wild, unshaven face under the old hat.

"Elaine," he whispered, backing behind the rock, "is it him?"

I nodded.

"Are you absolutely sure?"

"Absolutely certain."

"Well, then, this time we mustn't lose him!" Peter's eyes were bright with adventure. "He can't see us in that mist, and we can track him by that funny clatter and his boots on the stones. We must follow him, Elaine, and see where he goes. Come on!"

There was nothing to do but follow, for I was far

too frightened to go home alone; also, I did not want to desert Peter. So I set off behind him, shivering with cold and fear. The man did not go down the lane. He turned off to the left across the boggy uplands, which made things far more difficult and dangerous, for there were no covering trees, and we had to keep a good distance away. We could just see his dim, shambling figure striding along, and we knew that if he turned around he would certainly see us.

He was walking very fast, for he was wearing big boots that squelched through the mud and bog moss, but for me in my small sandals it was much harder going. Twice I sank right down into black water over my ankles and, to my terror, Peter seemed to be getting ahead of me. I dared not call in case the man should hear and turn around.

Thicker and thicker grew the mist; it seemed to be building white walls all around us. I began to panic and to run wildly to catch up with Peter, but it was treacherous ground to run on. I caught my foot in a clump of thick heather and fell headlong. For a moment I was too stunned to move, and when at last I scrambled up again, I was quite alone in a white, silent world. Peter and the man had completely disappeared.

Well, he couldn't be far ahead. Surely all I had to do was run fast for a few minutes, and Peter's sturdy figure would loom up in front of me. But I forgot that we were following no road, and I'd lost all sense of direction. Peter might have gone anywhere, and the more I ran, the farther away from him I might be going, out into the lonely night to be swallowed up by the thick darkness and the mist. I stretched out my hand in front of me and found I could hardly see it.

There was only one thing to do, and that was to turn around and try to find my way back to camp. So I turned around and trotted off, shivering and crying, in the direction I thought I had come from. I suppose I walked for hours, and I realized that I must have gone around and around in circles. I was almost too tired to feel frightened anymore, and at last I sat down hopelessly on a little rock and gave myself up for lost.

The ghostly white mist was changing into gray, and I knew that night was falling over the hills. I wondered dully what had happened to Peter, and I tried to think what to do next. If I sat still on that wet rock, I was sure I would freeze to death. It seemed years since I'd sat on the sunny slope with Philippa. We had talked about the path of life. It wasn't the path of life I wanted just then—it was the path back to camp! It was the first time since being lost that I had been able to think properly, for I had been stupid with cold and panic before. But now into my weary, numbed brain came a new thought. Was the Lord Jesus still there beside me in the mist? Was I still in His presence? If so, why was I so dreadfully afraid?

"Show me the path, Lord Jesus," I whispered, and just saying His name seemed to warm and strengthen me and give me new courage. I got up and went on walking, not knowing where I was going, but with a strong feeling of being led. I felt the presence of the Good Shepherd with me, who long ago, I remembered, had gone out to the mountains to seek for one lost sheep, and how much more now would He seek for a lost child? New peace came into my heart, and I suddenly felt safe.

I could not say how long I walked. Sometimes I called out, but my voice sounded so small in the blackness that I gave it up. At last I found myself scrambling on loose stones and I realized I was back in the old quarry, near the ruined house with the blackened walls and the empty, staring windows.

My heart gave a leap of terror, which passed quite quickly. According to Johnny, someone lived in these ruins, but anyone at that moment was better than no one. Surely anyone on a night like this would take pity on a lost little girl and take her home.

I seemed to have reached the top of the stone pile, and my eyes, peering in the darkness, could make out a solid mass ahead of me. The next moment I slipped and, because there was nothing but loose stones to hold on to, I went on slipping and slipping, faster and faster. The next thing I knew I was lying half in the water and half out of it, with my leg all twisted around the wrong way.

I tried to move, but the pain made me feel sick. Once again, in desperation, I cupped my hands around my mouth and called, "Help! Help! Oh, please help me!" And in my heart I cried, *Oh, Lord Jesus, I can't go on any longer. Please send someone now!*

I lay holding my breath and listening. At first I could hear nothing but the wind and the water, but after a few minutes I heard the noise of slow, shuffling footsteps coming from inside the ruined house.

"Help!" I shouted again. "Oh, please, help me!"

I saw the glow of a lantern framed in one of the window gaps and heard the creaking of the broken door. Someone was certainly coming, and whoever it was, it was an answer to my desperate cry for help. I had not been forsaken. I had been led to this strange place, and now someone was being led, slowly, stumbling over the stone toward me. I could hear the heavy boots kicking the stones and splashing through the water, and a voice I had heard before said, "Who's there?"

Why did that voice send shivers down my spine? I caught my breath and seemed to lose the power to answer. The next moment he had raised the lantern above his head and was looking down into my face, and I was looking up into his—a haggard, sick, unshaven face—a face that I knew.

20

The Rescue

Well, I'll be!" said the man, as we stared at each other by the eerie light of the lantern. "Seems as though I can't shake you off, doesn't it? And what are you doing here?"

I could not speak at first, I was so terrified. Was this the answer to my prayer? Had I been left to the mercy of this dreadful thief? I could only gaze up at him, my body rigid with fear.

Perhaps he understood how I felt, for he spoke again quite gently, and the wild look seemed to fade out. "Now, now," he said. "There's no need to look like that. I'm not going to hurt you. You're hurt already, aren't you?"

"Yes," I whispered between dry lips. "I think . . . I think I've broken my leg."

"Is that so?" he said, kneeling down beside me and scanning me again with the lantern. "Well, I'm going to carry you into my house, and then you can tell me what you're doing here."

I screamed with pain as he lifted me out of the stream, and clung to him desperately. He smelled of beer, and the weight of me seemed to exhaust him, for he breathed heavily as he plodded back to the ruin. He had left his lantern outside, but I felt myself being lowered very gently onto a mattress, and it was not pitch dark, for some ashes still glowed red in the stone fireplace.

He left me and returned in a moment with the lantern. His face looked white and weary. He sat for a moment at the bottom of the mattress, holding his head in his hands. Then he turned around and stared at me again.

"Well," he said at last, "what do you think you are doing, spying on me like that?"

"I wasn't spying," I whispered pleadingly. "I . . . I didn't know you lived here. I got lost in the mist, and I fell over in the quarry."

"You were following me," said the man, "you and that boy up on the moor. I saw you before you saw me. The boy followed me right up to the pub."

I was silent, for I had nothing to say. I just lay there, wondering if he would kill me.

A wave of anger suddenly seemed to pass through him. "I could do away with you here, now, if I liked," he said, shaking his fist at me. Then, seeing my terror, his anger seemed to pass as quickly as it had come. "But you needn't be frightened. I'm not going to hurt you at all. I had a little girl myself once. She turned out bad, and God only knows where she is now, but she was an innocent little thing like you once. Now I suppose if you're lost, every policeman in the district is out on the mountains looking for you. Got me into a pretty fix, haven't you?" He sat staring into space, as though trying to make up his mind what to do.

"If you could go and get Mr. Owen from the Davies's farm," I faltered at last, "he'd take me home. I promise I'll never, never tell. No one would ever know I knew you."

"Oh, the boy's seen to that," said the man flatly. "I watched him and that parson chap go up to the police station together. I thought I'd be safe here one more night. It was too dark for a getaway just then. Besides, I've nowhere to get away to. I'm finished . . . down and out. I'll be better off in prison when the bad weather comes, so here goes."

He rose to his feet but still seemed uncertain what to do next. He made sure I was as comfortable as possible. "So long," he said. "Put in a good word for me when I'm taken. Remember I did my best for you." Then he was gone.

The pain in my leg was dreadful. I lay in the dark, staring at the tiny glowing patch of ashes. I was not afraid of this man any longer, for if he was a thief, he was a kind thief, and I did not want him to go to prison. But I realized that by saving me he was giving himself up, and I felt terribly sorry about it.

I must have lain for a long time half dozing. A storm had blown up. Fortunately the corner in which

I lay was roofed over and dry, but the wind howled through the spaces in the wall. I was first shivering, then burning, and not very sure where I was. I was parched with thirst and lost in great blackness. I had somehow forgotten about Jesus, but He was still there, and I realized that not for one minute had I been alone. The rain was still beating down, and the night was pitch black, but the love of God shone around me like light. "Fullness of joy," I whispered to myself. "I'm not afraid anymore . . . and I believe someone's coming."

I strained my ears to listen. Above the rain and the rushing water, I could hear men's voices, and the next moment I saw the steady glow of a storm lantern through a window gap. The old door creaked, and the room was aglow with lantern light, and there was Mr. Owen looking almost as ill and haggard as the man who followed him.

"Elaine, my poor little girl!" he cried, kneeling down beside me. "Thank God I've found you! Are you hurt? Can you tell me?"

I nodded. "My leg," I murmured. "And I'm thirsty. Please, can I have a drink of water?"

He had already pulled a knapsack off his back containing warm clothes and food and a flask of tea. I could not eat anything, but the tea was delicious. Now that he was here, I wanted nothing in the world but to go to sleep. The storm was still raging outside, and there was nothing to be done but stay there till morning.

I slept fitfully, as the pain kept waking me. I lay drowsily watching Mr. Owen and the man. They had blown up the dying ashes into a warm blaze and were sitting talking.

"You'll always be a hunted man, even if you do get away," I heard Mr. Owen say earnestly. "Far better to get it over with. They're after you now, and if they catch you running away, they'll be hard on you. If you give yourself up, they'll be easier on you. And I'll stand by you and tell them what you did for our little girl. It won't be as it was before. I'll be waiting at the end of it, with a job for you, and a home for you to come to. Get it over, man, and start again. You're starving, aren't you? Have a sandwich."

I drifted back into an uneasy sleep, and when I woke again a pale light was stealing into the wretched room. The rain had stopped, and the sky over the stone heaps was faintly golden. The man lay fast asleep on the floor in front of the fire, and Mr. Owen sat with his head in his hands, keeping watch over both of us.

Hearing me stir, he rose stiffly to his feet and came over to me. He looked worn out with sleeplessness and anxiety. He had more hot tea ready and fed me like a baby. Examining my leg very gently, he said, "We will have to get hold of a stretcher and an ambulance, Elaine. I think your leg is broken."

I shut my eyes. I cannot remember clearly what happened after that, but after a time I realized that Mrs. Owen was sitting beside me, and Mr. Owen had gone. Then there seemed to be a great many people in the ruin, and I felt a sharp stab of pain as I was lifted onto a stretcher, and after that I knew I was being carried downhill, for it bumped and jolted, and I felt the sunshine on my face. Then we were all going somewhere in a car, but I was too tired to ask where. I was conscious of being carried indoors and seeing nurses gathering around me, and I kept putting out my hand to make sure Mrs. Owen was still there, and she always was, and I wondered what the family was doing without her. And then I felt a prick in my arm and knew nothing more for a very long time.

I was very, very ill, so I learned later, and nearly died. Not only was my leg badly broken, but the long hours spent running in wet clothes, the cold, the fall, and the fright had all been too much for me.

Whenever I woke, either Mr. or Mrs. Owen was there beside me. Once I woke from a bad dream and found Janet beside me, her face pale and tear-stained.

"Janet," I asked, suddenly clear and sensible, "why are you crying? Am I going to die?"

Poor Janet! She never knew how to pretend or to say anything that wasn't the exact truth, so she answered my question simply. "I don't know, Elaine. They say you might. But you needn't be frightened—you'd go straight to Jesus."

"I'm not afraid," I answered, struggling for breath to explain. "Fullness of joy . . ." Then the mists closed around me again, and I fell asleep.

Then suddenly all the faces disappeared, and there was just one that was there all the time—my mother's face. At first I hardly recognized it, for it was no longer pretty and carefully made-up. It was pale and frantic with great dark circles under the eyes. And when I cried out in my dreams, she would clutch hold of me, and I felt her fear almost as strong as mine. Somehow we both seemed lost in the mist together. So night followed day, and day followed night, and I dreamed and cried and woke and dreamed again.

And then suddenly I woke up properly and knew I was not dreaming any longer. It was very early morning, for the windows were gray. I raised myself on my elbow and called the nurse, who came over to my bed at once.

"Where's my auntie?" I asked her. Surely they hadn't all gone and left me!

"Your mother's here, sleeping in the side ward," said the nurse kindly. "I'll get her at once."

Mummy was at my side in a few moments, in her night clothes. She looked old and tired and dreadfully frightened, and I had a strange feeling that it was me who should be helping her.

"Hello, Mummy," I said calmly. "I'm better. Did you come because I was ill?"

"Oh, Elaine," cried my mother, putting her arms around me and bursting into tears. "Are you really better? I thought I was going to lose you, and I was so dreadfully frightened!"

"I wasn't afraid," I answered. "I'd have gone to be with Jesus. But now I'm going to get better instead. Please give me a drink, Mummy. I'm really thirsty."

The nurse arrived with a tray of tea and biscuits for my mother, and she took my temperature and seemed delighted. My mother fed me, and I found I was hungry and ate two biscuits. Then, tired but still feeling cool and at peace, I lay holding her hand as the sweet summer dawn came creeping in through the windows, and the birds began to sing in the hospital garden.

21

The Path that Led Home

I soon began to feel quite well again, and my mother said she should be getting back to work. I was still in bed on the morning she left, and for the first time I brought up the subject of the Christmas holidays.

"We shall be leaving France in November, darling," she said, "and then it will be only another few weeks, and you'll be home for good. I'm already finding out about flats, and I'll get two weeks holiday over Christmas. What fun it will be to be together again!"

I lay very still. I did not want to hurt Mummy's feelings, but somehow she must understand. I wanted to see her on visits, but my home was here in the country now with Janet and Philippa; I could not go back and live in London. But I did not know how to explain and, being very weak after my illness, the tears welled up in my eyes and I felt my lips trembling.

My mother stared at me and went rather red. There was a long, uncomfortable silence.

"Don't you want to come home?" she asked in a light, hard voice. "Would you rather stay and have Christmas with the Owens? They seem very fond of you. It will be just as you like, you know."

It was the chance I had been waiting for, but somehow I could not take it—I wasn't sure if Mummy was angry or just sad, but in any case I was too nervous to explain anything. I lay there feeling miserable and twisting the sheets in my hands.

"Well," said my mother, "you've only to say so, and it'll be exactly as you like."

"I . . . I don't know. I'll ask Auntie," I whispered. "I'll tell you later, Mummy."

"Oh, very well," answered my mother coldly, "but make up your mind soon, as I must make my plans as well." She glanced at her watch and yawned. "I must be going soon. Well, good-bye, darling. Get better quickly. I'll be back in a few weeks."

She kissed me lightly and turned away. But the nurse stopped her at the ward door, and I caught a glimpse of her face and noticed tears on her cheeks. I buried myself under the bedcovers and cried and cried.

I'll ask Auntie to explain, I thought to myself. *She'll be able to make Mummy understand.* And with this I comforted myself and grew stronger every day, until one morning the doctor stopped quite casually at the bottom of my bed and said he thought I could go home the next day.

Waiting to go seemed to take forever—I was so excited. Mrs. Owen, Janet, and Peter came to get me, all looking almost as excited as I was. At last we were all driving through the gates and away into the world that I had not seen for nearly a month.

Mr. Owen, Blodwen, Johnny, Frances, Robin, Lucy, and Cadwaller were all at the gate under an amazing banner with the words *Welcome Home* stitched across it in uneven red letters, and the noise of their greeting must have shaken the parish. I was carried down the path by many loving hands and in through the front door, where another surprise awaited me. The table was laid for a party, and the room was full of red roses, while on the couch by the window lay Philippa, with her mother sitting beside her. Philippa was determined to be there on the great day.

It was a wonderful party, better than Christmas, so Johnny remarked. We had ham sandwiches, chocolate biscuits, fruit salad, and a big cake baked by Blodwen, frosted by Janet, and with "Welcome Home, Elaine" printed on it in silver balls by Frances. We talked and talked, because there was so much to say.

Then Mr. Owen told us about the thief, who might have escaped if he had not gone out in response to a cry for help. All night long, Mr. Owen had talked with him while I slept an uneasy sleep. The man told his pitiful story. He had had an unhappy childhood, then his wife had left him, taking with her the only person he had really loved—his little girl. He had already been to prison once and come out ill, without work, and without a friend in the world. Life had been a bitter, hopeless struggle ever since, and he was sick of it all and ready to give himself up. He fully admitted to the robbery.

So he and Mr. Owen had gone to court together, and the previous week he had been sentenced to three months' imprisonment. But he had gone quietly enough, knowing that at last he had a friend who would stand by him all the way through and be there waiting for him on the day when the prison gates would open for him. Mr. Owen had promised to write to him every week and visit him once a month, and already Mr. Owen was looking for a kind employer and a decent job for the man.

We sat silently for a minute, thinking of the poor man's unhappy life. I glanced around at the happy, healthy children, the good food we were eating, the warm clothing we were wearing, the yellow evening sunshine streaming in the window, and realized we'd been given very much.

I think we could have talked all night, but Mrs. Owen suddenly jumped up and said that I'd been up too long for the first day and must go to bed at once. So they all came to the bottom of the stairs to watch me climb up with my plaster-casted leg and wave good night to me.

Mrs. Owen helped me into bed and then went off to get me a last hot drink. It was wonderful to be back in my own little room and to know I would wake up in the morning and find Janet sleeping beside me. And then an unhappy thought came into my heart—suppose I had to leave it? Suppose I had to go back to London? Well, I wouldn't leave it; it was my home now, and Mummy had said I could do as I liked. Now was my chance to get things straight.

Mrs. Owen sat down on my bed while I drank my hot chocolate, and I decided to talk to her about it there and then.

"Auntie," I said abruptly, "I never want to go back to London. I want to stay here and have Christmas with you and go on going to school with Janet. Can you tell Mummy, because she said I could do what I liked, and she could always come up and visit me?"

Mrs. Owen looked very troubled, and this surprised me, for it had all seemed perfectly simple to me.

"I couldn't tell her," she said. "If you really want to stay, you must talk it over between yourselves. Of course, we all want you to stay very badly, and we will miss you dreadfully if you go. But you see, you are all your mother has got. Have you ever thought how lonely she would be without you?"

I was silent. I had not thought very much about her side of it. My own side mattered to me too much.

"I don't think we need to decide tonight," she said quietly. "We must think about it. But don't forget your special verse. The Lord Jesus has the path all planned out for you. Ask Him to show you very, very clearly where it is going to lead you, because only by walking in that path will you find fullness of joy."

She kissed me and left me, and I buried my head in the pillows and said my prayers. But I did not ask to be shown the path of life. I just said, "Please, please, let me stay here because I could never be happy again in London."

I grew strong again surprisingly quickly, and by October my cast was off, and I was able to go back to school. I could also climb the hill to visit Philippa again, and I looked forward to these visits, for she had really changed. She had asked Jesus to come and live in her heart, and since that day He had quite simply been teaching her that true happiness lies in making other people happy and by giving instead of getting. Day by day, she was putting up a brave, steady fight against grumbling and selfishness, and winning victories over her crossness and self-pity. She worked hard at her lessons now, and had learned to knit, and was always thinking of things she could do for other people. Mr. Owen used to visit her and tell her about the parish, and she had started to knit clothes for new babies and to write little letters and verses for people who were ill or in trouble.

It was on a clear, cool day toward the end of October that I was sitting on the windowsill talking to Philippa. It was nearly time to go home.

"Elaine," said Philippa suddenly, "when do you have to go back to your mother in London?"

The old fear leaped in my heart, for it was nearly November, and Mummy would soon be coming. But I felt sure it would be all right. After all, she had said I could do as I liked.

"I'm not going back," I answered. "Mummy said I could choose. I'm going to stay here. I could never be happy in London."

Philippa's clear blue eyes, which sometimes seemed to see much more than I wanted them to, were looking at me in surprise. "Well, I can't believe it!" she exclaimed. "You told me that if I belonged to the Lord Jesus, I could be happy with lame legs, and I believed you. And now you say that you couldn't even be happy in London. Having lame legs is far, far worse than living in London!"

Her words seemed to hit me, and I had no answer to give at all, but I tried to think of some excuse. "Oh, but if I went back to London, there'd be no one to teach me about Jesus," I stammered. "My mother doesn't know much about the Bible."

"Well, neither does mine," said Philippa firmly. "But she's awfully pleased I've stopped being so cross, and I told her it was knowing about Jesus. So now she thinks the Bible must be a very good Book, and she comes and reads it with me. But all the same, Elaine, I really do hope you don't go away because I shall miss you so much."

"Well, it isn't quite decided," I said slowly, rising to my feet. I wanted to get away and think things over. I said a hasty good-bye, but I didn't go home. I climbed to the lamb pasture and sat down on the roots of a huge beech tree. I could see a long way. Just below me were the woods, and beyond them the brown, plowed fields, then the purple-blue line of the sea, and the pale evening sky. This was my home, the land I'd learned to love. How could I leave it?

I turned and looked behind me. The hills seemed very close tonight, and on one of them I could see a lonely little path winding up over the rocks and twisting through the yellow bracken. It seemed to run right to the top of the crest and to meet the sunset.

"Lord Jesus," I whispered, "show me the right path.

I really want to know."

And, as I sat waiting for my answer, I began to think about my mother—my pretty, clever, capable mother, who went to France and gave parties and rushed off in airplanes and always seemed to know what to do and how to do it. And yet at the hospital she had been desperately afraid, and I remembered her frightened face and the funny feeling I'd had that Mummy was lost in the mist, and I must put out my hand and lead her home. And there was no one else. The Owens all had one another, but Mummy had only me.

I turned and went downhill, limping a little. Across the shadowed fields I saw two figures coming toward me. Mrs. Owen had started out to look for me, and plump Lucy was toddling beside her. We met by the first beech tree, and I slipped my hand in hers.

"There's a letter from your mother," said Mrs. Owen a little hesitatingly. "She's coming to see you on Saturday to talk things over."

I looked up with the light of certainty on my face. "Good," I said. "I'm glad she's coming. I'm going back to London at the end of term to live with her."

There was a moment's silence. Perhaps Mrs. Owen was waiting for me to explain, but I'd said all I had to say.

"Did you find out? Is it the path of life?" she asked softly at last.

I nodded.

"Then you'll find fullness of joy," she said, stooping to pick up Lucy. And hand in hand we strolled home through the dark fields, and the lights shone out in a cozy glow from the vicarage windows ahead of us.

More Excellent Reading from
Patricia St. John and Moody Publishers

Treasures of the Snow

A beautifully written and engaging story that captures the innocence of childhood, and the joys found in the little things. Learn what the healing power of repentance and forgiveness can bring as we heed our Savior's voice in our lives.

ISBN: 978-0-8024-6575-7,   Paperback

The Tanglewoods' Secret

In a struggle to overcome her fiery temper and selfish spirit, Ruth is led to the discovery of a very important Shepherd who can and does teach her (and others) how to be good. The story contains beautiful and uplifting examples of what can happen when we let ourselves be found by Him.

ISBN: 978-0-8024-6576-4, Paperback

MOODY
Publishers™

From the Word to Life

1-800-678-8812 www.MoodyPublishers.com

The Secret at Pheasant Cottage

Lucy has lived with her grandparents at Pheasant Cottage since she was a little girl but she has a dim memories of someone else. Who was it? What are her grandparents hiding from her? Lucy is determined to find the answers but it turns out to be harder than she expected.

ISBN: 978-0-8024-6579-5, Paperback

Star of Light

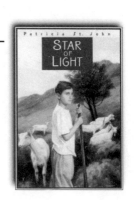

Star of Light is a beautiful, yet sensitive fictional book (though it seems like non-fiction). Set in North Africa, this book is about a little boy named Hamid and his younger sister, Kinza who is blind. It is the story of a little boy's love for his sister and how he rescues her from being sold into an inevitable life of abuse.

ISBN: 978-0-8024-6577-1, Paperback

MOODY
Publishers™

From the Word to Life

1-800-678-8812 www.MoodyPublishers.com